Rehearsal or Reality?

"Tamera," Lamar said as they drove through the darkness. "I'm really glad we're in the play together."

"Me, too," Tamera said. "You don't know how happy I was when you came through the auditorium door. I thought I was stuck with Roger as Romeo."

"Now, that would have been interesting," Lamar said, laughing.

"That would have been gross," Tamera said.

Lamar pulled up outside Tamera's house. "One good thing," he said. "Being Romeo and Juliet gives us a great excuse to practice. Although I don't think we really need any practice, do you?" He took Tamera's chin in his hand and kissed her gently on the lips.

"Good night, Juliet," he whispered.

Sister Sister

★ STAR QUALITY ★

JANET QUIN-HARKIN

A
MINSTREL®
BOOK

Published by POCKET BOOKS
New York   London   Toronto   Sydney   Tokyo   Singapore

A MINSTREL PAPERBACK *Original*

 A Minstrel Book published by
POCKET BOOKS, a division of Simon & Schuster Inc.
1230 Avenue of the Americas, New York, NY 10020

Copyright © 1997 by Paramount Pictures

ISBN: 0-671-00285-6

First Minstrel Books printing April 1997

10 9 8 7 6 5 4 3 2 1

A MINSTREL BOOK and colophon are registered trademarks of
Simon & Schuster Inc.

Printed in the U.S.A.

★ STAR QUALITY ★

Chapter 1

✥

"Tia? Where are you? Guess what!" Tamera Campbell closed the front door behind her, crossed the entryway, and stood in the empty living room. She looked around in surprise, expecting to see her twin sister, Tia Landry, sitting there. "Tia?" Tamera's voice echoed through the house. "Where are you?"

Silence answered her. She went through to the kitchen to see if Tia was fixing herself a snack, then she checked to see if Tia was watching TV.

This is really weird, Tamera thought. They had taken the same bus home from school half an hour earlier. Tia had headed in the direction of their house, while Tamera had lingered on the corner, chatting with some friends. Now there was no sign of Tia. "Tia? Have you been kidnapped by aliens?"

Tamera called out, only half joking. She couldn't imagine where Tia could have got to.

Now that she thought about it, she remembered that Tia had been acting weirdly on the bus, too. When Tamera had been kidding around with their friends, Tia had hardly said a thing. Instead she had stared out of the window and Tamera had had to nudge her that it was time to get off.

I should have asked her if something was wrong, Tamera thought guiltily. She had been having such a good time, hanging with the group, that she had hardly noticed when Tia walked on ahead. What if Tia had a really big problem and had gone somewhere to be alone?

Then she smiled at her dumb panic. Tia must be up in their room, probably with headphones on, listening to the new CD she had bought the day before. Tamera took the stairs two at a time and threw open the bedroom door.

"Oh, there you are," she said in relief. Then she paused. Tia wasn't listening to music. There was total silence in the room. The drapes were drawn, and Tia was sitting on her bed, cross-legged. Her eyes shut, not moving. Tamer tiptoed around her sister, but Tia's eyes didn't flicker. Tamera remembered her kidnapped-by-aliens quip. Now it didn't seem so funny. She was beginning to wonder if Tia's body *had* been taken over by aliens.

"Tia?" Tamera asked again, a little nervously. "Are you okay?"

Tia opened her eyes and glared at Tamera. "You

made me lose my concentration," she said. "I was just getting something."

"What are you doing?"

"Concentrating."

"On what?" Tamera came over and perched on the end of her sister's bed. "Are you trying to have a psychic experience? Cool! If you're trying to dream up your dream boy, dream one up for me, too, while you're at it."

Tia smiled. "If you really want to know, I'm waiting for inspiration."

"You're going to write a song or a poem? That's cool, too. I could cut the CD for you. Roger could be my backup singer."

"Tamera, I'm trying to come up with the perfect idea for the science fair," Tia said patiently.

"Oh." Tamera tried not to let her face show the disgust she felt. How could anyone waste that much time and effort over a science fair? She would never understand her sister in a million years.

Tia drew her knees up to her chest and sat there, hugging them. "I've decided to enter the citywide science fair. It was announced at my science club meeting today. The first-place winner gets five hundred dollars, Tamera. And even better than that, the winners are on TV and get loads of publicity."

"I can think of easier ways of getting on TV," Tamera said. "You could join a protest outside the mayor's office. You could even get on a game show."

Tia smiled and shook her head. "I don't want the publicity. I'd hate to be on TV, but it would make colleges notice me, wouldn't it? I'm going to need all the scholarships I can get, if I want to go away to a good school, and I really do."

Tamera nodded as if she understood, but inside she was trying to imagine what it would be like when she and Tia went to different colleges one day. There was no way that she'd get into the kind of college Tia would go to. They'd become so close in the past year. It would be terrible to be apart again.

"So you see," Tia went on, "I have to come up with something really outstanding if I have a chance of making it to the final round of the science fair, and right now my mind is a blank. I thought if I sat in the dark long enough, and let my thoughts just flow freely, I'd come up with a fantastic idea."

"I got a blue ribbon once for showing how plants need air and water," Tamera said. "I put one plant in a jar with no air holes and one in a jar with no water and they both died. Mind you, all the plants I tried to grow died anyway, even if they got air and water, so I guess that doesn't prove much."

Tia gave her a pitying look. "Tamera, last year's science fair winner practically cured cancer all by himself. Does that give you a hint that I have to come up with something pretty special here?"

"Don't look at me," Tamera said. "You know my science skills don't go any further than the dead plant in the jar. But I don't think that sitting in the dark and thinking is going to do it. What you need is some sort of diversion—like going to a movie, for example. I came to tell you that Denise just told me that movie is playing at the Plaza—you know, the one we wanted to see, where the four girls go to college together and promise to be best friends forever and then they steal one another's boyfriends?"

She looked at Tia for recognition. "Denise and I thought we'd go tonight. Want to come with us?"

Tia shook her head. "No, thanks."

"Tia, every scientist knows that laughter stimulates the thinking chemicals in the brain. And the movie is supposed to be super funny. And Marcia overheard Sean Peters saying that he was thinking of going tonight. You did want to find a way to meet Sean Peters, didn't you?" Tamera had noticed her sister watching the hunky junior whose locker was just down the hall from theirs.

Tia shook her head again. "I don't have time for diversions in my life right now. No movies, no cafes, no boys."

"You might as well check into the nearest convent," Tamera said. "You're only fifteen years old, Tia. You're supposed to be having fun, getting out there, meeting guys. You have the whole rest of your life to be serious and boring."

"Maybe I think the science fair will be fun," Tia said hotly.

Tamera raised her eyes to the ceiling. "I don't know what happened with our genes," she said, "but somehow along the way all the fun DNA went into me and all the nerdy DNA went into you."

Tia was staring at Tamera so hard that finally Tamera felt uneasy. "What?" she demanded. "Do I have candy stuck in my teeth or something?"

"No, but you are brilliant."

"I am? In what way?"

"Tamera, you might have come up with the perfect project for me."

"I might?"

"Yeah! The DNA of twins."

Tamera took a step backward toward the door. "Hey, you're not messing with my DNA. I like myself just the way I am."

Tia laughed. "I'm not going to touch your DNA, Tamera."

Tamera was still looking suspicious. "I know you. You're going to grow up to be one of those mad scientists—you'll stop at nothing in the cause of science. The moment I fall asleep, you'll probably start sticking giant needles into my head to suck out my brain."

"I wouldn't need a giant needle, Tamera. It would only take a small pin to get into your brain," Tia said. "You really are clueless sometimes. What I'm going to do is see if any research has been done on the DNA of identical twins and then maybe write a paper on it."

"Oh," Tamera said. "No needles?"

"Absolutely no needles. You can rest in peace."

"Rest in peace? Couldn't you phrase that differently? It sounds like you're waiting for me to die so that you can cut my body up for science."

"Tamera, you're being really weird about this," Tia

said. "But you've started me thinking. It really would be great if I could get someone to analyze our DNA and see where we were different. Maybe if I went to the biology professors at Wayne State. Heather's parents would know who to ask."

She jumped up. "I've got to get busy right away. It's only two months until the science fair. I have to get to the library this very minute. Tell my mom where I am if I'm late for dinner, okay?"

She crammed a beret onto her head, snatched up her book bag, and ran down the stairs. Tamera heard the front door slam after her.

"Definitely weird," she said to her reflection in the mirror. "I'll bet she finds that our DNA doesn't match at all, at least not in the area of the fun genes."

She headed downstairs again, just as Tia's mother, Lisa Landry, came in the front door. "Hi, Tamera honey, is Tia up there?" Lisa called as she saw her. "Big fashion fair at the mall tomorrow. It's a great opportunity for me to show off my latest designs. I'm going to need her help, setting up my booth. And maybe she can help me with sales, too. A cute girl modeling one of my creations has to get me noticed, doesn't it?"

"Good luck," Tamera said. "If you want Tia, try the library. That's where she'll be for the next two months. She's doing research for her latest project."

"What now?" Lisa asked.

"She's entering the citywide science fair," Tamera said. "And she's decided to do research into twin DNA."

7

"Say what?" Lisa asked.

"You know—the DNA of twins. How it matches and how it doesn't."

Lisa shook her head. "I haven't a clue what you're talking about."

"Me neither," Tamera said. "I'm just repeating what Tia told me."

A big smile spread across Lisa's face. "That's my baby, the scientific genius," she said. "Now she's going to win a science fair. She just does one thing after another to make me proud of her. Isn't she something?"

"Oh yes," Tamera said. "She's certainly something."

Lisa was already heading in the direction of the phone. "I can't wait to tell people about this," she said. "Run that DNA thing by me again."

"Don't look at me. I'm the dumb one, remember," Tamera said coldly.

Lisa looked at her with understanding. "I'm sorry, honey. I didn't mean to hurt your feelings. But I can't help being proud of my daughter because she keeps on doing all these fantastic things, can I?" She looked at Tamera, then gazed into space. "I wonder if she'll need a new outfit for the science fair. Maybe I could design her one. Those scientists always look so geeky. She'll be the only fashionable genius there." She walked toward the kitchen, leaving Tamera standing at the bottom of the stairs watching her.

At the kitchen doorway she paused and turned back. "How about you, Tamera honey?"

"Me? Enter a science fair?" Tamera spluttered.

"No, for tomorrow. Can you come help me set up my booth? You won't have anything better to do, will you?"

"I guess not," Tamera said.

She went slowly back up the stairs.

"This is déjà vu all over again," she said to herself as she shut the bedroom door behind her. Now she had to look forward to another painful bout of Tia being Miss Wonderful. Lisa would tell everyone in the world how smart Tia was. People at school would stop Tamera to ask her if she was Tia's sister. Even her own father, who wasn't even Tia's relative, would be bursting with pride. And Tamera would feel like the stupid one again, the one who didn't matter, the one who wasn't special.

When is it going to be my turn? she asked her image in the bedroom mirror. But she couldn't come up with an answer.

Chapter 2

✑✑

Tamera's friends Denise, Sarah, and Marcia were waiting for her at the espresso bar in the mall, outside the entrance to the movie theater.

"Where's Tia?" Denise called as she waved to Tamera.

"Not coming," Tamera said. She pulled out a chair and sank into it.

"That's too bad," Sarah said. "I thought she was dying to see this movie."

"She's given up movies, boys, and cafes. That's what she told me," Tamera said.

"She's becoming a hermit?' Marcia said with a giggle.

"Worse—she's doing another science project," Tamera said, wrinkling her nose. She looked up and smiled as the cute waiter stood over her. "I'll have a double latte," she said, "with whipped cream on top and chocolate sprinkles. Oh, and one of those pastries to go with it."

"Tamera—I thought you said at lunchtime today that you were on a diet," Denise said.

"This is comfort food," Tamera said. "I need comforting."

"Why? What happened? You were laughing and joking when we left you a couple of hours ago," Denise said.

"Then I found out about Tia's science fair project," Tamera said.

Denise stared at her. "Run that by me again— you're depressed about your sister's science fair project? She's not making you do some of it, is she?"

"I don't think she'd do that. She wants to win," Tamera said. "I'm the dumb one, remember?"

"Oh, so that's what's wrong," Marcia commented. "You don't like your sister getting all the glory."

"I don't care if she gets the glory," Tamera said. "It's just that sometimes I'd like just a teeny little bit of glory, too."

"Then enter the science fair," Marcia said.

"Get real, Marcia," Tamera said. "I think it helps if you're *not* failing science."

"Then do something else," Denise said.

"Like what?"

"You're good at all sorts of things, Tamera," Marcia said encouragingly.

"Name one."

"You're great at flirting and coming back with

good answers to boys," Denise suggested, giving Tamera a wicked smile.

"I don't think they award too many prizes for flirting," Tamera said.

"You were great at basketball," Marcia reminded her.

"Yeah, but it's not basketball season for months and months yet," Tamera said.

"So go out for softball then," Sarah said.

Tamera shrugged. "It's too late for softball tryouts, and anyway, I'm okay at sports but not what you'd call a super jock."

"Then come and try out for the play with me on Monday," Sarah suggested.

"Oh no." Tamera shook her head firmly. "I'm not going through that again."

"What do you mean?" Denise asked.

"I went to tryouts with Sarah once before," Tamera said. "They wanted to give me the part of the cow. I was supposed to stand there in a cow suit and say 'Mooo.' Can you imagine?"

"Typecasting again, huh, Tamera?" Denise teased.

"It would have been a way to break into show business, Tamera," Marcia said. "You could have been udderly brilliant. Udderly—get it?"

Tamera was the only one who didn't smile. "It wasn't funny. It was awful, Marcia. They were all laughing at me. I nearly died of humiliation."

"But it will be different this time," Sarah said. "It's a drama club production of *Romeo and Juliet*."

"Oh, that really does convince me," Tamera said.

"We did that play last semester and I didn't understand one word. That Shakespeare guy writes in some foreign language."

"It is not. It's just old-fashioned English," Sarah said. "I think it's very beautiful."

"Oh, sure," Tamera said. "If it's English, how come I can't understand it? And the parts I can understand are very boring—a lot of old guys talking to each other. I got in trouble for falling asleep in English class."

"*Romeo and Juliet* isn't boring. It's very romantic," Sarah said. "Just think of it—they took poison and died for love in each other's arms."

"That's not romantic, that's stupid," Tamera said. "I wouldn't end up taking poison just because some guy ditched me."

"He didn't ditch her, Tamera. Their love could never be because they came from two families who were feuding."

"I know all about that," Tamera said, her face lighting up. "I've watched *Family Feud.*"

"Tamera, you're hopeless," Marcia said, giving her a friendly shove as the waiter came back with Tamera's order.

Tamera looked up at the waiter and smiled. "Thanks a million," she said. "You do that very well."

"Do what?"

"Carry the latte without spilling it."

"Uh—sure. No problem," he said, putting down the items quickly and hurrying away again.

"See? I am hopeless," Tamera said. "Now I can't even get guys to notice me. No talent whatever."

"I think you should try out for the play," Denise said. "That will be a great opportunity to meet guys. Let Tia get bogged down in her science project. You can be the one with the part in the play and a boyfriend!"

"Isn't it just all the dorky guys who go out for acting?" Tamera asked.

"Is Tom Cruise dorky?" Denise demanded. "Or Denzel Washington?"

"I meant at our school. I don't want to find myself surrounded by nerds."

"Trust me," Sarah said. "And when I tell you who's directing the play, I know you'll want to try out."

"Don't teachers always direct plays?"

"Not this one. Damien Baker is doing it as a senior project."

"Damien Baker? The one with the little mustache who looks like a young Will Smith?" Tamera shrieked.

"Now are you coming to tryouts?" Sarah asked with a knowing grin.

"Sarah, I don't get Shakespeare," Tamera said. "It would be a total waste of time for me to come to tryouts because I wouldn't have a clue what I was reading. Nobody else would understand what I was reading, either."

"There are small parts, too, you know," Sarah said.

"You could be a servant who comes on and bows and says, 'Here is your cloak, my lady.'"

"Even that will probably be in Shakespeare talk," Tamera said. "It will probably be something like 'But low, soft, I bringeth thy warmeth outergarment.'"

"See, you can say it," Denise said, grinning at Tamera.

"Only to you guys," Tamera said. "If I had to say that stuff in front of an audience my tongue would get all tied up in the *bringeth*s and *forsooth*s."

"They have nonspeaking parts, too," Sarah said. "They have to have townspeople and Juliet's friends, and they need people to help backstage, building the set and making costumes."

"Oh, that would definitely steal some of the glory from Tia," Tamera said dryly. "I can just see it now. 'Okay, Tia, so you won the citywide science fair and were interviewed on TV, but your sister helped paint that archway with twenty other people.'"

"It's not a contest, Tamera," Marcia said. "You're not in competition with your sister. You just have to have fun and be your own person."

"And I think you would have fun being in the play," Sarah said. "We have great cast parties, and we all go out for pizza after rehearsals, and some of the guys are such hams. You'd love it."

"I guess I could give it a try," Tamera said. "After all, what have I got to lose? And if I don't find myself something to do, Lisa will have me helping her at her fashion cart every weekend."

"Hurry up, Tamera. The show starts in five minutes," Denise said, getting up.

Tamera drained her drink and got up. "Who knows—maybe this will be my thing, after all. Make way, Tamera Campbell the famous actress is coming," she said. She crossed the mall, swinging her hips and trying to walk like a movie star. A group of teenage guys stopped and stared as she passed them.

"Did you see that?" she said as they went into the movie theater. "Maybe I have got what it takes after all. Did you see the way those guys turned and looked at me?"

"That's because you have a white mustache of latte, Tamera," Sarah said, getting a tissue out of her pocket to wipe Tamera's upper lip.

The others were giggling as they went into the movie. Tamera tried to smile, too, but she was feeling very down. The only time people noticed her was when she did something dumb. She sat there in the darkness, still feeling her face hot with embarrassment as she remembered how she had walked past those boys, wearing a big mustache of latte.

She didn't want people to think of Tia as the smart twin and her as the dumb twin, but that was what seemed to be happening more and more these days. She knew she wasn't as smart as Tia and never would be, but she wasn't stupid either. She just didn't enjoy things like science the way Tia did. But she remembered that she had done okay until Tia came along— she had never had any trouble making friends or getting involved in school activities. In fact—it came back to her suddenly—she had had the lead in the play back in third grade, hadn't she? Yeah—Tamera grinned to herself—she had been the head Pilgrim in the Thanksgiving story. She remembered how good it had felt, standing in the middle to take her bow, seeing her dad sitting there, bursting with pride, and everyone coming up to tell her how cute she was. . . . So maybe she did have star quality and acting talent and she had just kept them buried until now.

The preview of a really dramatic movie was showing. "Torn from each other's embrace in a world shattered by war," the announcer was saying. A man and a woman were hugging each other, and then the woman stood there at the window, watching him go. Tamera tried to match the grief on the woman's face. She tried to pretend she was Juliet, dying of a broken heart. She closed her eyes and let herself drift into a fantasy. She saw the amazement on everyone's face as she read at tryouts.

"Where have you been hiding?" Damien Baker asked her. "You're the most gifted actress I've ever seen."

And on opening night everyone rushed onto the stage after the show telling her how wonderful she was. Her arms were piled full of flowers, and a strange man tapped her on the shoulder. "I just happen to be a talent scout from Hollywood," he said, "and I'm going to make a superstar of you."

Then she was swept off to Hollywood in a private plane and she became a megastar. She came home in time to present the prizes at the science fair. Tia was standing on the podium, about to get the first prize, but when Tamera came in, someone shrieked, "There she is. That's Tamera Campbell!" and everyone rushed to her, leaving Tia standing all alone. Tamera pushed through the crowd and went up to Tia. Then she hugged her, making sure the cameras got her best side.

"Tia, I've missed you!" she exclaimed. "Congratulations on winning the science fair."

Tamera opened her eyes and had to laugh.

Let's stay realistic here, she told herself.

On the way home later, she thought about her fantasy. She didn't really want to be famous, did she? And she didn't really mind that Tia was the smart one. In fact she was proud of Tia and hoped she would win the science fair. All I want is something of my own, she decided. I just want to have fun and do my own thing. She still wasn't too sure that Shakespeare would be her thing, but she had to start somewhere. She would take a look at tryouts on Monday. And if she could see that the play wasn't for her, then she didn't have to go back.

I've got nothing to lose right now, she told herself. And who knows, maybe I'll discover the star quality I had when I played the Pilgrim.

Chapter 3

❀

"*A*rt thou sure that I looketh okay, forsooth?" Tamera asked nervously as she examined her reflection in the school bathroom mirror.

"You look fine," Sarah said impatiently. "You've asked me that a million times already. Now, let's get going or they're going to start tryouts without us."

"But do I really look like a Shakespeare person?" Tamera asked. "I went through my entire closet this morning, but this was the closest I could get to olden times. Do you think it sends the right image?"

Sarah looked at Tamera, taking in the long denim skirt, the crushed black velvet body suit with the big white lace collar and the black beret, jammed, as usual, on her forehead.

"Definitely the right image," Sarah said, "although

I'd ditch that hat. I don't think old-time women wore berets."

"You want me to take my hat off?" Tamera looked worried. "But you know I never go anywhere without my hat."

"I'm just saying it's not very old-world," Sarah commented. "Who cares what you wear to tryouts, Tamera. The director only wants to see if you can act, not what you wear."

"But it's important to me that I look right," Tamera said. "You really think I should take off my hat? My hair always goes crazy when I take my hat off. It's totally wild, see?" She took off her beret and ran a brush through her wild, dark curls. She tried to smooth them down with her hands, but the curls sprang back again.

Denise popped her head around the bathroom door. "Are you still in here, you guys? What's taking you so long?"

"Tamera's still not ready," Sarah said.

"You're not trying out for *90210*, Tamera," Denise said. "It's only the school play."

"But I don't know what to do with my hair," Tamera protested. "I can't leave it like this!"

"It looks fine, Tamera," Sarah said. "Quit worrying. I don't want to be the last one to try out. They've already made up their minds by then. I hope I get a speaking part this time. It was so boring last time being a statue."

"I hope I don't blow it," Tamera said, grabbing onto Sarah's arm. "I've never actually tried out for a play before. Last time I was in a play, they just gave me the lead."

Sarah looked startled. "When was that?"

"When I was the head Pilgrim, back in third grade," Tamera said. Without warning she grabbed Sarah's and Denise's arms and dragged them through the nearest door.

"What is going on, Tamera?" Sarah demanded. "Have you gone crazy?"

"You're hurting my arm, Tamera," Denise wailed. "And why are we standing in a social studies classroom?"

"Sorry, guys, but I thought I saw Tia at the other end of the hall," Tamera said.

"You're hiding from your own sister? Why?" Denise demanded.

"I don't want her to know that I'm trying out for the play," Tamera said.

"Why not? Is drama forbidden at your house?" Sarah asked.

"Think about it, Sarah," Tamera said. "If Tia knows I'm trying out, then she'll blab about it at home. Then my dad and Lisa will get all excited, and I probably won't even get a part. I hate feeling like a failure, so I'd rather not tell them until I know something."

"That makes sense," Denise said. She peered out of the room. "No sign of Tia."

"She must be in the library by now," Tamera said. "Okay, let's headeth in the direction of old Verona."

The girls linked arms as they marched down the

hall to the auditorium. Tamera pushed open the door, then collided with Sarah as she tried to go out again.

"I'm not doing this," she said. "Look how many people there are."

"Tamera, stop freaking out. You've got just as much chance of getting a part as anyone else," Sarah said.

"Oh sure," Tamera said. "They'll probably want me to be a cow of Verona."

"Shut up!" Sarah said, giving Tamera a playful punch. She pulled her down into a seat beside her. "Think positive. That's what I'm doing."

"Okay, listen up, people," a deep voice yelled. Talking died to a murmur as Damien Baker stepped out into the middle of the floor. There were several seniors with him, holding clipboards.

"Hi, everybody, my name is Damien," he said. "And I'm going to be directing this play, with a little help from the English faculty." He glanced over at Ms. Thomas, one of the English teachers, who was sitting off to one side. "I'm, uh, doing this as a senior project, and I've never directed a play before, so I hope you'll all help me along here."

"He certainly is cute," Denise whispered, nudging Tamera. Tamera nodded in agreement, not taking her eyes off Damien for a second. She was wondering if he had a girlfriend and how he would feel about dating a mere sophomore. She imagined Tia's face if she brought him home.

"We're going to have the first round of tryouts

today," Damien went on. "You'll all get a chance to read, and then we'll have callbacks tomorrow after school for those people who made the cut. Got it? Great. Okay, let's get started. I have to warn you before we get going that Shakespeare isn't easy. We're doing a shorter version of the play, but it's still hard. If you get a part, you're going to have to work your tail off. Are you with me?" He looked around. "Anyone who wants to escape, you'd better do it before we lock the doors."

There was some nervous laughter. Damien grinned, too. "Okay, so I'm going to call up one girl and one boy to read the famous balcony scene. When you come up, give your name to Maureen here. Right, let's start with you." He looked straight at Tamera.

"Me?" It came out as a squeak.

"Sure. Why not?" Damien smiled at her encouragingly.

Tamera stumbled to her feet. Her hands were shaking so much that she could hardly hold the script that the girl handed her.

"And how about—you," Damien said, pointing to the back of the auditorium.

"Me?" A voice asked.

Tamera froze in her tracks. She knew that voice well—too well. It was Roger, her pint-size neighbor, who was always bugging her, following her around and hoping for a date with her.

"Roger?" she demanded as he came running toward the stage, his dreadlocks bouncing. "What are you doing here?"

"I'm waiting to play Romeo to your Juliet, O light of my life," Roger said, beaming at her in delight. "I knew this day would finally come, when we would take up the roles destined to us—me Romeo, you Juliet."

"How did you know I was doing this?" Tamera asked, wrinkling her nose in disgust. "I didn't tell anybody, not even Tia—and by the way, if you tell her before I do, you're dead meat, Roger."

"I didn't know you were doing it, I swear," Roger said, taking a step back as she came toward him. "I was passing the gym and someone said there were tryouts, so I thought, why not? It must have been destiny that brought me here. And here I am, and here you are. Romeo and Juliet. Now, that's what I call fate."

"That's what I call disgusting and unthinkable," Tamera said. "My only hope is that I know you'd never in a million years be cast as Romeo. He's supposed to be tall and handsome, not shrimpy and weird looking."

"People were shorter in Shakespeare's time," Roger said. "I'd say I was the perfect height. Just the right height to gaze into your lovely brown eyes and take you in my manly arms and whisper sweet nothings in your ear."

"Excuse me, but could you whisper your sweet nothings some other time?" Damien said with heavy sarcasm. "We do have another fifty kids waiting to try out."

"S-sorry," Tamera stammered. "I'm still in shock at finding that I have to read with *him*."

"Do you want to read, or don't you?" one of the senior girls asked impatiently.

"Okay, I'll read," Tamera said. "Only I have to say in advance that I've never understood Shakespeare, but I'll give it my best shot." She held up the script, took a deep breath, and started reading. " 'But, soft! what light through yonder window breaks?' "

"Excuse me for interrupting, but that's Romeo's part," Damien said. "Wouldn't you rather try out for Juliet?"

Tamera heard giggles behind her.

"Romeo begins," Damien said. "You want to start us off, uh, Roger?"

"I'm ready, willing, and able," Roger said. He picked up his script and started to read.

" 'But, soft! what light through yonder window breaks.' Hey, wait a second here. Has this Romeo dude just broken a window? I didn't know I'd be playing a criminal."

Damien was trying to keep his cool. "Roger, the light is breaking through the window, not Romeo. Got it?"

Roger stared at his script. "I wish they'd written it in English," he said. "What does all this stuff mean anyway? Couldn't we rewrite it a little, so we'd understand it. I could say, 'Hey, Juliet, mama, I really dig you on account of you're such a hot babe.' "

"Roger, do you want to read or don't you?" Damien demanded, his voice rising dangerously now.

Roger read the lines so that nobody could understand what he was saying. Then it was Tamera's turn.

" 'O Romeo, Romeo! wherefore art thou Romeo?' " she read. So far so good, she thought. " 'Deny thy father, and refuse thy name; Or, if thou wilt not, be but sworn my love,' "—she looked up, trying to act as well as read—" 'And I'll no longer be a . . .' " She looked down and couldn't find her place. " 'A cap . . .' a cappuccino," she finished.

The whole auditorium burst out laughing. Tamera could feel her cheeks burning.

"Okay, so I blew it," she said, hastily handing her script back to the senior girl and rushing back to Sarah and Denise.

"So much for Tamera the star," she muttered. "I can't believe I said that. How could I make such a fool of myself? I might as well go home now."

"Wait for us," Denise said. "You really weren't doing too badly until the cappuccino disaster. It wasn't fair on you finding you had to act with Roger. That would have freaked anybody out."

Tamera sat there and tried to pretend she was invisible. Damien called up more people to read. It seemed that everyone was having a hard time with the words. At last he sighed and looked across the room. "This is going to be harder than I thought. Danielle, would you like to come read for us, please?" he called.

A tall, beautiful girl in a tight red dress strode across the room as if she owned the place. "Where do you want me to start?" she asked. She had a low, musical voice.

"At Juliet's first speech," Damien said.

Danielle picked up the book and started to read. The words just flowed out with no effort at all. When she closed the book, everyone applauded.

"At least we know who's going to be Juliet, don't we?" Tamera whispered to Sarah and Denise. "She actually reads it as though she understands it. And she looks great, too. Now all they need is a tall, gorgeous Romeo to go with her."

"Take a good look around," Sarah whispered. "Do you see any tall, good-looking guys here? I don't. And the ones that look okay can't read or have funny voices."

"We might find that Roger winds up as Romeo," Denise chuckled.

"Please—don't say that even as a joke," Tamera said. "Can you imagine? Gross!"

"I'd like to see Danielle's face if Roger winds up as Romeo," Sarah spluttered. "I get the feeling that she thinks she's pretty special."

"Well, she *is* pretty special," Denise said. "She looks great, she has a great voice, and she can act. What more could you want?"

"Not Roger as Romeo, that's for sure," Tamera said. "Okay, let's go home. So much for my short-lived career as an actress."

Chapter 4

❧

"Tamera, get over here!" Denise yelled, grabbing Tamera's arm as she stepped out of math class the next day.

"What? What's happened?" Tamera looked startled.

"They've just put up the callback notice, and you're on it!" Denise said excitedly.

"Me? Are you sure?" Tamera shrieked. "But I was terrible. Are you sure the notice doesn't say 'This is a list of people we never want to see again, ever'?"

"No, because that Danielle girl is on it, too," Denise said. "So is Sarah."

"But not you?" Tamera asked.

"It's okay," Denise said, shrugging it off. "I didn't really expect to be. I know my voice is no good and I'm way too shy. I'm going to sign up to work on scenery, and that will be fun."

"You were just as good as I was, Denise," Tamera said. "I don't understand. But I'm sure I'll just wind up as a townsperson anyway. I hope Sarah gets a speaking part. She was pretty good, wasn't she?"

"I thought so," Denise said.

"Oh no," Tamera wailed.

"What?"

"I didn't wear my Shakespeare outfit today. I didn't think I had a hope of being called back. Now look at me—jeans and a T-shirt—I look totally grungy. I wonder if I've got time to go home during lunch hour and change."

"You know you're not allowed off campus, Tamera," Denise said.

"I could say it's an emergency. I could call Tia's mom and get her to say it was an emergency."

"I thought you didn't want anyone to know you were trying out," Denise reminded her. "I think that would kind of give it away."

"Whoops! You're right, Denise," Tamera said. "I can't go home, because Lisa would want to know why. Okay, so I guess I'm stuck looking like this."

"I'm sure they won't choose you because of how you look," Denise said.

"I'm sure they won't choose me, period," Tamera said. "Maybe they've just called me back to get another laugh, in case I say something wrong again."

Denise grabbed her shoulders. "You have to start believing in yourself, girl," she said. "They must have thought you had something. If you really want to be in that play, then start telling yourself that you're a good actress. You saw the way that Danielle chick walked across the room. Be like her."

"You mean like this?" Tamera said. She oozed down the hallway and pushed past a group of freshmen, going through the door. "Excuse me, little people," she said in a sexy voice. She turned back to Denise. "How am I doing, dahling? Am I just mahvelous?"

"Tamera, watch out, you're going to—" Denise began, but it was too late. Tamera spun around, only to bump into a group of senior guys.

"Hey, girl, what's your problem?" one of them demanded.

"Sorry, I didn't see you," Tamera said, which she realized sounded pretty stupid, because they were all on the football team and very large.

"You need glasses or a white cane, honey," another of the guys said with a chuckle.

Tamera shrank against the wall until they had passed. "Denise, am I destined to make a fool of myself everywhere I go?" she asked. "Now I'm not even sure I want to go to callbacks. I know they'll want me to play a cow again."

"Of course you have to go," Denise said. "Tamera, what's wrong with you? You used to be one of the most confident people I know. Back in grade school you used to believe you could do anything. Remember when you were the head Pilgrim?"

"That was before Tia came into my life. Now I feel like second best all the time. She does everything better than me, Denise. She's smarter than me, she's more creative than me, she's skinnier than me, even her hair stays in place better than mine. I feel like there has to be just one thing I can do better than her."

"She does work awfully hard, Tamera. She's always in that library, studying. And you've done a lot of goofing off in your life. When have you ever really thrown yourself into something you want to achieve?"

"The pool," Tamera said, with a hurt look on her face.

"Excuse me?"

"I threw myself into the pool when I wanted to learn how to dive."

Denise smiled. "I meant, when have you ever studied really hard to do well? That's why Tia succeeds more often than you do."

"Well, thank you, Ms. Counselor," Tamera snapped. "You want to tell me what else is wrong with me now?"

"Tamera, I didn't mean to upset you," Denise said. "I wanted to make you feel better."

"Oh, that sure has helped a lot, Denise. I feel wonderful now," Tamera said. She started to walk away down the hall. Denise ran to catch up with her and grabbed her arm.

"What I was trying to tell you was that Tia is probably no smarter or more creative than you are. She just works at things. So if you really wanted to work hard, you could be just as good as she is."

Tamera gave Denise a pitying look. "Denise, get

real. Tia actually likes physics. She enjoys discussing the big bang theory of the beginning of the universe. Does that tell you something here? Have you ever known me to get excited about math or science? Have you ever known me to understand math or science? Right. That proves my point, I think. Tia is smart and I'm not."

"Okay, so she's a little smarter, in a scientific way, but that doesn't mean she's more creative."

"She got a better grade than me in art. She learned to play the piano just by fooling around with it."

"Okay, so maybe she's a little more creative. But she doesn't have your personality."

"People don't laugh at her, you mean?"

"Would you shut up!" Denise said, giving Tamera a shove. "Think positive, Tamera. Believe that you're going to get a part in this play and that good things are about to happen to you. Say 'I can do it, and what's more, I'm going to do it.' "

"I can do it, and what's more, I'm going to do it," Tamera said. Then she repeated it loudly. "I can do it, and what's more, I'm going to do it!"

"Well, good for you," a boy said as he went past.

Tamera rolled her eyes to the ceiling. "Doomed," she muttered.

All afternoon Tamera thought about the tryouts. Should she go or shouldn't she? Was she just wasting her time? Would she just make a fool of herself again if she went? And if she didn't go, was she passing up her one chance to do something without Tia? She got into trouble in social studies because she didn't hear the teacher ask her a question.

"Daydreaming again, Tamera?" he said.

I'll show him, Tamera thought. Wait until I'm a famous actress.

After school she was heading for the bathroom to fix her hair when Tia came up behind her.

"Just the person I've been looking for," she said. "Tamera, you have to help me."

"Do what?" Tamera asked.

"Come with me to the hardware store."

"You've switched to shop?" Tamera asked.

"No, I need stuff for my science fair project."

"See, I knew it. You're building an operating room to suck out my DNA."

"Tamera, will you stop talking like that," Tia said. "I've decided to make a giant model of a DNA thread, but I'm going to need you to help me carry all the stuff home."

"When do you need to do this?" Tamera asked.

"Right now. I want to get started on it tonight."

"Sorry, but I'm busy right now."

"No, you're not," Tia said. "You were going to the bathroom to fix your hair. That's not busy."

"But I have something to do after I fix my hair."

"Like what?"

Tamera remembered that she didn't want Tia to know about the tryouts. "Something important."

"Like what?"

"I've . . . uh . . . promised to go shopping with Denise. She wants me to help her pick out a new dress." Tamera blurted out the first thing that came into her head.

"I can't believe you just said that!" Tia exclaimed.

Neither can I, Tamera thought. How dumb can you get?

"You're saying that it's more important to you to go shopping with a friend for a stupid dress than to help your sister win a science fair?"

"I promised Denise, Tia. Would you want me to break a promise?"

"Then go some other day with Denise. Tell her it's an emergency. She'll understand."

"I'm sorry, Tia, but she'll be waiting for me. I said I'd meet her at the mall. There's no way to get in touch with her," Tamera babbled on blindly.

Tia was looking at her oddly. "Oh, I get it," she said. "You don't want to help me because you think the science fair is dumb. You don't want me to win, do you? Fine, see if I care. I'll do the project without your help." She ran off down the hall and out through the doors, leaving Tamera standing there, feeling terrible.

She was still standing there, staring at the empty doorway, when an arm came around her shoulder. "There you are, my little Juliet," Roger's voice said in her ear. "Your Romeo is ready, willing, and able to escort you to the auditorium."

Tamera eyed him coldly. "Let me point out a couple of things here, Roger," she said. "First, I don't have a hope of getting Juliet. Second, you don't have a hope of getting Romeo. Third, I wouldn't let you walk down the hall with your arm around my shoulder, even if I were Juliet and you were Romeo, which you won't be. And fourth, if you don't take your hand from my shoulder right now, I'm going to sock you one."

"Okay, okay. I get the message," Roger said. "But I think you're making a big mistake. It's always a good idea to get on the good side of the star when you're in a play—and I aim to be the star of this one."

"I can't think what as, Roger," Tamera said, shaking herself free of him. "As far as I know there are no jackasses or dogs in the play."

Then she strode ahead of him as fast as she could walk. Once inside the auditorium she slid into a seat next to Sarah.

"Hi," she said.

"What happened to you?" Sarah asked. "I was looking for you all over."

"A close encounter of the really repulsive kind," Tamera said. "Roger tried to walk down the hall with his arm around me."

"Gross," Sarah said.

"He has some strange fantasy that he's going to be the star of the play."

"That boy needs a serious course in reality one-oh-one," Sarah said.

"Tell me about it," Tamera said. "He seemed to think that I'd get Juliet and he'd get Romeo."

Sarah put her hand over her mouth to stop laughing out loud. "Like I said—dreamworld," she said.

"Everyone knows that Danielle will get Juliet. And if they can't find anyone better for Romeo than Roger, we're in big trouble."

She broke off as Damien and his assistants came into the auditorium. "Welcome back, everybody," Damien said. "Today we decide who plays what, but everyone here is going to be in the play for sure. And if you only get to be a townsperson or a servant, and you don't even say a line, you're still important. People will be watching you. And the way you act on-stage will help the audience believe that they're not in Detroit anymore."

"Until they come out and find their hubcaps ripped off," a voice from the back made everyone laugh.

Damien grinned, too. "Okay," he said, consulting his clipboard. "We talked this over last night, and we need to hear most of you read again. We've made up our minds about a couple of people, and we don't need to hear them. Danielle, would you come here, please?"

Sarah nudged Tamera. Danielle got up and walked up onto the stage with a smirk on her face.

"Danielle, we all know that you sound and act great," he said. "So we'd like you to be the nurse."

There was a stunned silence, then Danielle blurted out, "Excuse me? I don't think I heard right. I thought you said you wanted me to be the nurse."

"Uh-huh. We want you to play the nurse," Damien said.

"The nurse?" Danielle shrieked. "You want me to

be the nurse? Are you out of your minds? The nurse is old and fat and ugly. Look at me—do I look the part?" She stood there, glaring at him. "I'm the best actress you've got, Damien," she said. "This just isn't fair."

Damien cleared his throat nervously. "Look, Danny, we know you're the best actress here. The nurse is a very hard part. That's why we had to give it to you—you're the only one who could do it."

"Gee, thanks a lot," Danielle snapped. "And Juliet? Pardon me if I'm wrong, but she's not an important character in this play?"

"Very important," Damien said, "and we were planning all along to give you Juliet."

"So why didn't you?" Danielle demanded coldly.

Damien shrugged. "The more we thought about it, we decided it wasn't right for you. Juliet is a very young, innocent girl. She's only thirteen, Danielle. She's never even dated a guy. You're seventeen and you've . . ." His voice trailed off.

"Dated lots of guys?" Danielle asked, fixing him in an icy stare.

"That and your voice is too old for Juliet." He looked around the room. "She has to come across as young and clueless."

Suddenly Tamera realized he was looking at her. "Tamera, we'd like to try you as Juliet."

For a moment Tamera thought she hadn't heard right, but everyone else was staring at her, too.

"Me?" Tamera could hardly get the word out. Then she said, "But I was terrible," at exactly the same moment that Danielle said, "But she was terrible."

Damien smiled. "You didn't exactly blow us away, I'll admit," he said, "but that was because you didn't have a clue about what you were reading. But you sound right, and you look just like we imagined Juliet would look—all wide-eyed and excited about the world. Do you think you could do it?"

"I-I'll give it a try," Tamera managed to stammer.

"Great," Damien said. "Then let's move on to Romeo. We have a slight problem here. None of the guys who read yesterday were exactly what we had in mind."

"What you mean is that they really stunk," a girl muttered from the back, making everyone laugh.

"They weren't, uh, exactly what we were looking for," Damien agreed. "So we're going to let everyone have a chance to read again. And we have to choose an understudy for the major roles, too, so give it your best shot."

Tamera sat there in a daze while other kids got up and read. She still couldn't believe what was happening to her. She had the lead in the play! She was going to be Juliet! Just wait until she told them at home. Just wait until she saw Tia's face.

Chapter 5

✑✑

*A*fter everyone had read, Damien and his helpers got together and did a lot of whispering. Sarah nudged Tamera. "Congratulations," she said.

"I still can't believe it," Tamera whispered.

"Neither can anyone else," Sarah whispered back. "Especially not that Danielle girl. Look at the way she's glaring at you."

Tamera grinned. "If looks could kill, they'd be carrying me out in a pine box right now," she said. "All the same, I do feel bad for her. She was the best one. It's not her fault that she looks—"

"Too old and sexy?" Sarah finished for her.

"I knew my cluelessness would pay off some day," Tamera said happily. "I guess I must look clueless and that was what they wanted."

"They're having a hard time deciding who's going

to be Romeo," Sarah said. "I don't blame them. All the guys were pretty hopeless."

"That Peter guy wasn't too bad," Tamera said. "But he looks totally nerdy. He blushed every time he read a line."

"At least Roger was terrible again," Sarah said.

"Juliet doesn't exactly have to kiss any of them, does she?" Tamera asked, looking around in disgust. "There is nobody in this room I'd like to kiss, even a pretend kiss onstage."

"Of course," Sarah said. "Didn't you know she has several passionate love scenes?"

"She does?" Tamera flicked through the script. "Where?"

"Just kidding," Sarah said. "It's Shakespeare. All they did was sigh and keep saying I love thee. You're safe."

"Phew," Tamera said.

Damien and his crew stopped discussing and looked up. "We're still having problems trying to choose Romeo. We asked some more people to show up today, but since they haven't, I suppose we'd better go ahead with what we've got. Roger, would you read Romeo for now?"

"No!" Tamera gasped. She grabbed Sarah's arm. "It can't be true. Tell me it's not true. I'm Juliet and Roger is Romeo? It's my worst nightmare."

Roger sauntered down the aisle with a big smile on his face. He stopped in front of Tamera. "What did I tell you, my little flower?" he said. "It was destiny that finally brought us together. Romeo and Juliet—just like it was always meant to be, Tamera."

"The only good thing about being Romeo and Juliet is that they both die before they can get together," Sarah said, giving Tamera a dig in the side.

"It's lucky that we live so close to each other," Roger went on happily. "I can come over every evening and we can practice the love scenes together. Maybe you could get your dad to build a balcony outside your bedroom window so I could practice climbing up. It wouldn't be too hard for me. I've already had enough practice climbing up the drainpipe to peek in your window."

"Roger, you're disgusting," Tamera said. "If you really are going to be Romeo and I don't wake up from this nightmare soon, then we rehearse in school and nowhere else. Touch me and die."

Roger smiled to himself as he faced Damien. "Just a little lovers' spat," he said. "She's really crazy about me. But she's kind of shy about showing affection in public."

Tamera was just trying to come up with a witty put-down to this last remark when the auditorium door opened, sending in a breeze that scattered papers. Everyone looked in the direction of the door. A tall, lean boy stood there, dressed in a letter jacket and comfortable ripped jeans.

"Sorry, Damien," he said. "I just got your message on my answering machine when I got home. I hope I'm not too late."

"You're not too late, Lamar," Damien said. "I'm

real glad you showed up. Get over here and meet people." Then he added under his breath, "We were getting pretty desperate here."

The boy walked up onto the stage with the easy grace of an athlete. Damien turned to the rest of the kids. "Everyone, this is Lamar Jones. He's been in several plays here. I asked him to come try out, but he told me he didn't have time to do this play because of baseball. Then I called him again last night and begged." He and Lamar grinned at each other. "I'm real glad you came, buddy."

"Yeah, the Pistons tickets did the trick," Lamar quipped.

Tamera noticed he had a wonderful smile. His whole face lit up, and his eyes really sparkled. Her heart was beating fast as she watched Lamar talking to Damien. She heard Damien say, "So you'll give it a try, that's great. I owe you one, buddy." He turned back to the waiting cast. "I think we finally got ourselves a Romeo," he said.

"Hey, wait a second," Roger complained. "I thought you just said I could be Romeo."

"I said you could read Romeo for now, Roger," Damien said. "But all along we were hoping that Lamar would do it. He's a terrific actor."

"Aw, come on," Lamar said.

"You are," Damien insisted. "You'll make a great Romeo."

He turned to look at Tamera. "Tamera, would you come here, please? I'd like you to meet your Romeo. Romeo, I'd like you to meet Juliet."

Tamera could feel Lamar looking at her with surprise as she walked forward.

"Hi," she said shyly.

Lamar was looking confused. "What happened to Danielle?" he asked. "Did she decide not to try out?"

"Danielle's here and she tried out," Danielle called from the audience seats. "She's the nurse."

"The nurse?" Now Lamar looked even more surprised.

"I'm supposed to be the only one who can play old and crabby convincingly," Danielle said in an icy voice.

Lamar grinned. "Typecasting again, huh, Danny?"

"Not even funny," she said.

Tamera was standing there, feeling very uncomfortable. She wondered if everyone else felt that Danielle should have been Juliet and she was some kind of imposter. She was sure they didn't think she'd be good enough for Juliet. She found herself wondering the same thing.

"This is Tamera," Damien said. "We're going to give her a try as Juliet."

"Hi, Tamera. How's it going?" Lamar said, and gave her that wonderful smile. He turned back to Damien. "Maybe I owe *you* one, buddy."

The way he said it made Tamera feel all warm inside.

"We'll post the rest of the cast tomorrow morning," Damien said, "and we'll give you a rehearsal schedule. We only have six weeks of rehearsal so everyone's going to have to work very hard. If you accept a part, I don't want to hear any excuses for not knowing your lines or for missing rehearsals. Are you with me?"

Everyone got up and headed for the exits. Tamera was still standing beside Lamar.

"I guess we'll be seeing a lot of each other, huh, Tamera?" he asked.

Tamera nodded. Somehow she couldn't make her mouth obey her to speak.

"See ya at rehearsal then," he said, and gave her a friendly wave as he headed for the door with Damien.

Tamera rushed over to Sarah and grabbed her arm. "Did you see that? If I'm dreaming, don't pinch me, because I don't ever want to wake up."

"He certainly is cute," Sarah said. "If I'd known you were going to wind up as the star, with the cutest guy in the room, I would have shut up about tryouts. Maybe they would have chosen me as Juliet and I'd be rehearsing with Lamar."

"Sorry," Tamera said. "I'm just as stunned as you are right now. I can't wait to get home and tell everybody. I might have a sister who's the brain of the century, but I'm the star of the play!"

The bus seemed to take forever. Tamera had to stand, crushed against the other passengers. It was already hard enough to breathe from excitement, and Tamera found that her head was spinning when she finally fought her way to the exit at her stop. She ran all the way down the block and was out of breath by the time she threw open the front door.

"Hey, everybody, guess what?" she yelled.

Her father, Ray Campbell, was sitting in front of the TV, watching the news. Lisa was pinning some fabric at the table. They both looked up at Tamera, and their faces were not friendly. Tamera stopped in her tracks. This wasn't how she had pictured the scene at all.

"What?" she demanded. "Why are you looking at me like that?"

"Tamera, I need to speak to you," Ray said. "I've just heard something very upsetting. You behaved in a very selfish way to your sister this afternoon."

"Yes, Tamera," Lisa added. "Tia came home very upset and told us that you refused to help her carry stuff for her science fair. The poor baby was exhausted, trying to bring home all those supplies on the bus alone."

"I'm surprised and upset, Tamera," Ray went on. "We're family and we should do everything we can to help one another. Tia said that you wouldn't help because you were going shopping with a friend. That is no excuse."

"Don't be too hard on her, Ray," Lisa said. "I suppose I can understand how she feels. It's kind of hard when Tia is always doing something exciting and getting all the praise. Maybe Tamera felt that she didn't want to help Tia get the glory anymore."

"You could be right, Lisa. I hadn't thought of that," Ray said. "Maybe Tamera is putting her negative feelings into negative actions and—"

"May I speak before you two psychoanalyze me?"

Tamera interrupted. "I didn't help Tia this afternoon because I had something important to do of my own."

"I don't think that shopping is important, Tamera," Ray began, but Tamera went right on.

"It wasn't shopping. It was something I didn't want to tell you guys about because I didn't want to get your hopes up until I knew."

"Knew what, honey?" Ray asked.

"I tried out for the school play," Tamera said.

"You did? Good for you," Lisa said. "And did you get a part?"

Tamera nodded. She took a deep breath. "I got the lead. I'm Juliet in *Romeo and Juliet.*"

Ray and Lisa both looked stunned. "You're kidding," Ray said in a shaky voice. "You got the lead in the school play?"

Tamera nodded.

"You got the lead in the play?" Ray was yelling now. He looked at Lisa in delight. "How about that, huh? My baby got the lead in the play. She's a star." He ran over to Tamera and hugged her. "I'm so proud of you, honey. I always knew that good things would happen to you someday. I always knew you'd find your talent somewhere."

Lisa came over to Tamera, too. "This is great news, Tamera. I'm happy for you, too, baby."

At that moment Tia appeared at the top of the stairs. She looked down and saw Ray and Lisa both hugging Tamera.

"What's going on?" she asked. "You're hugging her because she ditched me and went shopping?"

"She didn't go shopping, Tia," Lisa said. "She didn't want to tell us what she was really doing." She nudged Tamera. "Go on, tell your sister."

A beaming smile spread across Tamera's face. "Guess what, Tia? I have the lead in the play. I'm going to be Juliet in *Romeo and Juliet*."

Tia's eyes opened wide. "Are you serious? Wow, Tamera, I never dreamed that—"

"That I could do anything well?" Tamera asked.

"I didn't mean that," Tia said. "I just never imagined you'd be a great actress. Especially not in Shakespeare."

"Me neither," Tamera said. "But I guess the director saw something in me that I didn't know I had."

"I'm so excited," Tia said. "That is so cool." She ran down the stairs and threw her arms around Tamera. "Why didn't you tell me you were trying out? I'd have come and rooted for you."

Tamera shrugged. "I didn't know if I'd be any good. I didn't want you guys expecting big things of me and then me feeling like a failure if I didn't make it."

"But you got the lead, Tamera," Ray said. "You've never had any drama lessons. That must mean you're a natural-born actress."

"I guess so," Tamera said shyly. "I've finally found something I can do well. And you won't believe the other fantastic thing that happened to me as well—"

"You got drafted by the Pistons? You've been chosen for Miss America? You're replacing Katie Couric on the *Today* show?" Tia teased.

"Even better than that," Tamera said, her eyes shining. "I am Juliet, and you'll never guess who's going to be Romeo—Lamar Jones. Do you know who he is?"

"Tall guy who wears a letter jacket? He's got a really cute smile?"

"That's the one."

"Tamera—he's gorgeous. I didn't know he was an actor as well as an athlete. Wow, I'm truly impressed, and jealous, too. Imagine doing all those love scenes with Lamar."

"I feel like I've died and gone to heaven," Tamera said. "For once I'm not just going to be known as Tia's sister."

"That's right," Tia said. "People will stop me in the halls and ask me if I'm the sister of the star."

"Sister of the star!" Tamera echoed happily.

Lisa put an arm around both of the twins. "I'm so proud of you guys I could burst," she said. "The scientific genius and the acting star. I can't wait to tell the world." She went over and picked up the phone. "Who do I call first? Family or the press? Maybe it would save time if I just rented a billboard along the freeway." She looked at their faces and laughed. "Just kidding," she said.

"I've got a better idea," Ray said. "Go upstairs and

get changed, and I'll take you all out for a fancy dinner."

"Now you're talking," Lisa said. "Forget about 'Say it with flowers.' I like 'Say it with food.' "

Tamera and Tia were laughing as they walked up the stairs together. Tamera felt so happy that she was about to burst.

Chapter 6

@@

*A*fter school the next day Tamera went to her first rehearsal. She wore her favorite black velvet vest and matching velvet hat, along with a purple miniskirt and white shell. That outfit always made her feel good, and she wanted to look like a star. She tried to feel like a star as she took a deep breath and walked into the auditorium. Lamar was already standing on the stage, talking to some of the other guys, and he smiled at Tamera.

"Hi," he said. "Know your lines yet?"

Tamera's mouth opened in horror. "Al-already?" she stammered. "We were supposed to learn our lines last night?"

"You bet," Lamar said. "I've got all mine down pat."

"*All* your lines?" Tamera said. "You know all your lines?"

Lamar grinned. "Psych!" he said. "Damien will give us at least one more day."

"Shut up," Tamera said, laughing with relief. "I'm not going to believe another word you say, Lamar Jones."

Danielle came up to Lamar and put her hand on the back of his neck. "So, Lamar, honey, what about Trisha's party on Saturday? You'll be there, won't you?"

"I might," Lamar said. "I haven't made up my mind yet."

"I'll be there," Danielle said smoothly. "Does that make up your mind for you?"

Tamera wanted to say something clever and witty that would take Lamar's attention away from Danielle, but she couldn't think of anything. She could only stand there feeling helpless. *At least she doesn't get to act the love scenes with him,* Tamera told herself.

Damien arrived with his helpers and went around handing out schedule sheets. "Take a look at the schedule before we get started," he said. "You'll see we don't have any time to fool around. I expect you to know your lines for act one by the end of next week, act two by the end of the week after, and act three by the third week. After that, no more books."

Tamera started flipping through act 1. *That was a lot of words to learn in a week! But I'll get the feel for it during rehearsals,* she told herself. *Most of it will just come naturally. Especially doing the balcony scene with Lamar.*

"Okay, let's get started on a read-through," Damien said. "I expect you've all had a chance to look over your parts, so let's see if we can go all the way through without stopping."

Tamera felt herself getting hot and uncomfortable. She'd been so happy the night before that it had never occurred to her to study her part. She remembered how bad she had been at pronouncing the hard words. They started reading. Juliet wasn't in the first two scenes, and Tamera tried to look ahead to what was coming. But then she was scared of losing her place.

They came to her first scene, and she was glad she had only short lines to read. This is going okay, she thought, feeling herself relax. She watched with secret admiration as Danielle read her first big nurse's speech. Even sitting down and reading from a book, she made herself sound like an old woman. I bet she would have done Juliet just great, Tamera found herself thinking.

" 'Wilt thou not, Jule?' " Danielle finished.

Tamera looked at her own line. " 'And stunt thou too, I pray thee, nurse,' " she read.

She looked up as she heard giggles.

"Can't you even read a simple line?" Danielle demanded.

"That's *stint*, Tamera, not *stunt*," Damien said kindly.

"I don't know what either of them mean," Tamera said.

"When she says 'stint' yourself, she really means she wants her to shut up," Damien explained.

"Oh, okay." Tamera went on reading. Damien had to stop and help her, almost every line she read. She realized that she didn't have a clue what she was saying, ever. And she didn't have a clue what anyone else was saying. The lines were just a lot of old-fashioned words, joined together without any meaning.

By the end of the read-through, Tamera was feeling scared. Other people had had trouble with their words, but Lamar had breezed through his lines as if he knew what he was saying. In fact he sounded great. Somehow she had to sound as good as he did someday. How am I ever going to learn all this? she wondered. For the first time it was beginning to hit home that having the lead in the play meant a lot of work. And Tamera had never worked really hard in her life.

"Do you want to stop off for a soda or a coffee?" Sarah asked her when the read-through was over. "I'm really thirsty, aren't you?"

"Sorry, but I have to get home and study, study, study," Tamera said.

Sarah looked surprised. "Study, you? When did you ever study, study, study? Is this the new, improved Tamera?"

"That's right," Tamera said. She flicked through her script. "Look at all these lines I've got to learn. And I'm hopeless at learning things. I was the last one in the class to learn the Pledge of Allegiance in first grade."

Sarah nodded in sympathy. "Yeah, now I'm kind of glad I'm only a servant. I don't how I'd ever learn all those lines."

"I don't know how I'm going to either," Tamera said. "I really need someone to explain what the words mean as I go along." Then she clapped herself on the forehead. "Wait a second—what am I worrying about? I've got my own resident Miss Encyclopedia Brain. I'll get Tia to help me."

"That's a great idea," Sarah said. "She can say the line and you can repeat it. You'll learn really fast that way."

"I hope so," Tamera said. "I don't want to look like an idiot. Oh, well, 'bye, Sarah. Gotta run. Wait a second, what I mean is I musteth to haste away for night falleth and I am missing ye rerun of *Roseanne*."

"Hey, Tamera, how did the first rehearsal go?" Lisa asked as Tamera burst through the front door.

"Fine, thanks," Tamera said. "Where's Tia?"

"Upstairs working," Lisa said. "Do you want a snack before dinner? We're having lasagna, but I've made you a big salad. You have to start dieting now that you're a star. Those pounds show up onstage, you know."

"Thanks, but I don't have time for a snack. I've got to study," Tamera said.

Ray's head poked around a door. "Was that Tamera talking?" he asked in surprise. "I thought it sounded like my daughter, but she just said she had to study, so I thought I was hearing wrong."

"Very funny, Dad," Tamera said. "I have a zillion lines to learn. See you later."

She took the stairs two at a time. "Hey, Tia," she yelled. "Let's get to work. You've got to help me—" She pushed open the bedroom door and then skidded to a halt.

"Whoa!" she yelled.

Taking up most of the bedroom floor was a big tower of what looked like giant building blocks. "Watch out!" Tia warned. "It's not glued yet. I'm just trying it out."

"What is it?"

"It's going to be my model of a DNA strand," Tia said. "It's not in the correct order yet. I'm just seeing if the blocks will fit together. DNA strands twist, so that's going to make it hard to do."

Tamera was still staring. "When you said a model, I pictured something that went on a tabletop," Tamera said. "Not something that takes up half the house."

"It has to be big enough so that everyone can see my display at the fair," Tia said. "Once I can make the blocks stay put, then I have to make them different colors and arrange them in the right order."

"Now that you've built your tower, I really need your help," Tamera said. "I have all these lines to learn by the end of this week, and I don't even understand what most of the words mean."

Tia made a face. "Gee, Tamera, I'd like to help you, but I've still got a lot of work to do on this model."

"It looks fine to me," Tamera said.

"How would you know what DNA is supposed to look like?" Tia said, smiling. "Tamera, I have weeks of work before I get the blocks looking right and arranged in the right order for what my paper is explaining. And I have a huge pile of hard books to read before I can start writing the paper."

"But I can't learn all these lines without you, Tia," Tamera said. "I don't even understand what I'm reading. I thought that you'd read the line first and then I'd say it after you."

"I really would like to," Tia said, "but I just don't have the time, Tamera. This project has to be perfect for the science fair."

"In that case," Tamera said in a hurt voice, "could you take your project somewhere else. I need to practice my lines."

"You could do that downstairs."

"No, I couldn't. I have to read them out loud, or I'll never get the hang of them."

"You can read them out loud downstairs."

"How can I? My dad and Lisa will want to watch the news on TV."

"Then go out in the backyard. I don't know," Tia said.

"Hey, this was my room before it was your room," Tamera snapped.

"Well, right now we share it," Tia answered.

"Then do your crummy DNA model in your half of the room. You're taking up my side of the floor as well."

"Okay, I will," Tia said. Carefully she dragged her tower of blocks across the floor until it was directly in front of her bed.

"Is that better?" she asked. "Just make sure you don't come on my side of the room and disturb my blocks."

"Okay," Tamera said. She got out her script and sat on her bed. She started reading through her lines, muttering them to herself in a low voice. Tia looked up in annoyance, went to say something, then shut up.

" 'I'll look to like, if looking liking move,' " Tamera muttered. " 'I'll look to like, if looking liking move. I'll look to like if looking liking move.' "

"Tamera!" Tia complained. "It's very hard for me to work with that noise going on."

"I can't help it. I have to get this right. 'I'll look to like, if looking liking move.' What does that mean anyway? This is all so stupid!"

"I'm sure you'll get the feel for it when you act with the others," Tia said kindly.

"I hope so," Tamera said. "I'm getting freaked out about this, Tia. I was so excited when I got the lead. I never stopped to think that I'd have to learn all this stuff. Now I'm scared that I won't be able to do it and I'll look like a fool."

Tia went over and sat beside her sister. "You can do it, Tamera. You just have to concentrate hard."

Tamera sighed. "I just hope I can get it right. I know that the other kids in the play don't think I deserved to get Juliet. I don't want to prove to them that they were right."

"Tamera, you have to believe in yourself," Tia said. "They wouldn't have chosen you if you weren't the best actress. So tell yourself that you're a great actress and you can do it. You just have to be prepared to work hard."

"I knew there had to be a catch somewhere," Tamera said. "I'm not good at working hard, Tia. At least, I'm great at working hard for about two minutes, max."

"It's up to you, Tamera," Tia said. "If you really want this badly enough, then you'll do what it takes. I want to win the science fair, and I'm prepared to work my tail off to do it. You have to be prepared to stay up working till midnight every night if necessary. You have to sacrifice like me—no movies, no TV, no boys, no shopping, no cafes . . ."

"No TV at all?" Tamera asked worriedly. "How about a quick trip to the mall on weekends? I have to get my shopping fix once a week."

"It's up to you," Tia said. "Like you said, you have a lot of lines to learn."

"Okay, I'll work hard," Tamera said. "I just wish that I had someone to work with me. It would make it so much easier."

"Tamera, get down here, there's someone to see you," Lisa's voice called up the stairs.

Tamera ran out of the room. Roger was standing at the bottom of the stairs, looking up hopefully.

"What do you want, Roger?" Tamera asked coldly.

"I've come over to help you, my little Juliet," he said. "I thought we could go through our lines together."

"But you're not Romeo, thank goodness," Tamera said.

"No, but I'm his understudy, which means I have to be perfect in case he meets with a terrible accident just before the performance and I have to go on in his place. So I need to rehearse with you, so that I'll know how and when to take you in my strong, masculine arms and—"

"Forget it, Roger," Tamera said. "I'm having a hard enough time trying to learn my own lines, without having to keep running to the bathroom to throw up at the thought of acting with you. Go work with Juliet's understudy, because if anything happens to Lamar, there is no way I'm going to be on a balcony with you. So good night and get lost."

She ran back up the stairs. Tia was lying on her bed, shaking with laughter. "What were you just saying about wanting someone to work with?" she asked. "See, the answer to your prayer. I can't think why you sent him home."

"Not funny," Tamera said as she picked up her script again.

Chapter 7

∞

By Friday, when they were supposed to be word perfect in act 1, Tamera was sure that she knew her lines. She had said them over and over so many times that she kept muttering them all night in her sleep. In fact Tia had gotten out of bed and nudged her a couple of times. "You're muttering again," she had said.

But as they took their places for the first act, Tamera was feeling good and grinned at Lamar. She got through the scene with the nurse, by concentrating very hard on every word. " 'I'll look to like, if looking liking move,' " she said, stressing every word with large pauses in between. Then she pumped her fist and said, "Yesss!"

"You're not supposed to break character in the middle of a scene," Danielle complained.

"But that was a hard line for me and I got it right," Tamera answered. "I was happy."

"So what do you want, a medal?" Danielle asked dryly.

"Get on with it, please," Damien said.

The play went on until Juliet's first scene with Romeo. Suddenly Tamera was very conscious of Lamar standing there beside her, saying lines about lips and kissing. She tried to think of her next line, but her mind was blank.

" 'Good person,' " she began. "No, wait a second. I mean, 'Good pilgrim.' Yeah, that's right. 'Good pilgrim, you do wrong yourself too much.' No, hold it. I goofed. Let me do it over. Okay. 'Good pilgrim, you do wrong to your hand.' No, forget I said that. 'Good pilgrim, you do wrong your hand too much.' "

"Is this going to happen with every one of your speeches, Tamera?" Damien asked. "I need to know, because we'll need to book the theater for the whole night and provide pillows and breakfast, because the play will take at least ten hours."

"Sorry," Tamera said, feeling embarrassed and stupid.

"I told you you had to know act one by today," Damien said. "If you don't want the part, just say so. There are plenty of other girls here who do."

"I'm really sorry," Tamera said again. "I did work hard to learn my lines. And I thought I knew them. It's just that I don't know what I'm saying so they don't mean anything to me. They come into my head and right out again."

Damien nodded. "I understand," he said. "This is hard stuff. I've done a couple of Shakespeare plays, and I still have to keep going to Ms. Thomas to find out what the language means. But you have to keep going if you flub a line. When you're all dressed up as Juliet, you can't stop and say, sorry, I got that word wrong. Let me do it over."

The other actors giggled nervously. Tamera tried to smile, but her insides were clenching themselves into knots. She really wanted to be Juliet so badly, and she was just about to blow it. Then Lamar touched her arm.

"If it helps, we could work on our scenes together," he said. "It's much easier if you have someone to act with."

"That would be great," Tamera said, gazing up at him. "But don't you have enough to do with this and baseball?"

"I guess I could make some time," he said. "I don't play baseball after it gets dark. I could come over to your place some evening, maybe."

"Okay. That would be great," Tamera said. She tried to act cool and not look as if this was about the most wonderful thing that had ever happened to her. "How about tonight? I don't think anything's happening at my house." She managed to say it without her voice shaking.

"I guess I could stop by tonight," Lamar said. "Where do you live?"

As Tamera collected her things at the end of practice she saw Maureen, one of the senior girls, go up to Danielle.

"Do you know what I just overheard?" Tamera heard her say.

She saw Danielle glance up sharply in her direction. Then she heard Danielle say, "Don't worry about it. How could he be interested in her? He's just trying to help her out so that she doesn't make the rest of us look bad." She leaned closer to Maureen, so that Tamera had to strain her ears to hear. "If you really want to know, he told me that he finally decided to come to Trisha's party tomorrow."

"And you're going to be there?"

"Of course," Danielle said. "Why else do you think Lamar said he'd come?"

Tamera ran out and hurried home. So many thoughts were flying around inside her head that she almost missed her bus stop.

"Everyone, I've got a great idea," she yelled as she stepped into the living room. "Why don't you all go to a movie tonight? You've been working hard all week. You deserve a night out."

Ray looked up from his newspaper. "I'm working tonight, honey," he said. "One of my men is sick, and I've got to drive the limo."

"Oh, okay," Tamera said. That wasn't bad news at all. At least her dad would be out of the house and he was the main one that she worried about. "How about you and Tia, Lisa. Don't you feel like a mother-daughter night out?"

"I wouldn't mind it at all, but Tia's not leaving

that DNA of hers," Lisa said. "She's stuck up in that room until she gets it right."

"Oh," Tamera said. "I suppose you don't feel like going to the movies alone?"

Lisa looked at Tamera suspiciously. "Okay, what's happening here? I get the distinct feeling that somebody wants us out of the way, for some no good reason!"

"It's a very good reason, Lisa," Tamera said. "One of the kids from the play is coming over to rehearse with me, and I don't want anyone listening in on us until we've got it right."

Lisa's face relaxed. "Oh, in that case, why don't I just take the portable TV up to my room? Then you can have the living room to yourselves."

"Thanks, Lisa, you're the greatest," Tamera said. She ran up to Tia, who was kneeling beside the DNA tower in the bedroom.

"Hey, Tia, guess what," she said in a low voice. "You'll never guess who's coming over here tonight—Lamar Jones."

"No!" Tia looked up. "Nice going, sis."

"He's coming over to rehearse with me. He actually suggested it, which must mean something, right?"

"Like what?"

"That he likes me? He wants a chance to be alone with me?"

"He wants to get your scenes right?" Tia suggested.

Tamera sighed. "That's what that snobby Danielle said. She thinks Lamar is hot for her. She said he was only helping me because he felt sorry for me and he didn't want me to screw up his scenes." She sat down heavily on her bed. "I wish I knew more about boys, Tia. I wish I knew what they were thinking."

"You probably don't want to know what they're thinking, Tamera," Tia said with a smile.

"I really want Lamar to like me," Tamera said, ignoring her, "but I don't know how to show him I'm interested. When I'm with a guy I really like, I just clam up. And when I open my mouth, I say something really dumb."

"Working together on a play is good, Tamera," Tia said. "That's a shared interest. That's the best way to develop a friendship."

"I wish his coming over really did mean that he liked me," Tamera said. "He's going to a party with Danielle tomorrow night. I wish I had the nerve to crash it."

"Your dad probably wouldn't let you go," Tia said.

"You're right. Ohmygosh, I've only got two hours to get ready before he comes. What should I wear? How should I do my hair—up and sophisticated or down and innocent? You've got to help me get ready, Tia." She opened her closet and started grabbing clothes, then hurling them around the room as she spoke. "Fuzzy sweater and jeans with—no, too young. Body suit and black leather—no, too old. Pink sweater and . . ."

Tia looked up and glared at Tamera as she removed a pink fuzzy sweater from her DNA model. "When you've finished playing at Goldilocks and the Three Bears, I am trying to get some work done.

Just be yourself with him, Tamera. And stop driving me crazy."

Tamera opened her mouth to say something else, then she looked at Tia and said, "Okay," in a small voice. "I guess I can keep wearing what I've got on now. Maybe I should study my lines some more. Oh, and one thing, Tia."

"What?"

"Spy on us and die."

"As if I would, Tamera. Give me a break. My DNA is way more important than watching you and Lamar."

Right on the dot of eight the doorbell rang. Tamera leaped for the door. Lamar was wearing a light blue Lions sweatshirt, which made him look even more handsome than ever.

"Hi," he said with an easy smile.

"Hi." Tamera could hardly get the word out.

"Ready to get a lot of work done?" he asked, bringing her just slightly back to reality.

"Okay," she said. "I'm ready."

"Let's do that first scene when Romeo and Juliet meet," he said. "Do you think you know it?"

"In theory," Tamera said. "When I'm all alone in my bedroom, I can say it through just perfectly. When I'm standing out there with all those people, it goes again."

He looked down at her with warm, brown eyes. "Tamera, that's what actors do—they perform in front of a lot of people. You're going to have to get used to that. Focus on the person you're acting with and tune everyone else out. Let's start."

He said his lines to her. He got as far as "My lips, two blushing pilgrims, ready stand to smooth that rough touch with a tender kiss."

Tamera found that she was looking at his lips and wondering what it would feel like if . . .

"Tamera, your line," he said.

"What? Oh, right." The line had gone clean out of her head. "What do I say?"

"Tamera, concentrate."

"I'm trying. It's not easy," she said. I hoped for too much, she told herself. He only came here to rehearse. It doesn't worry him at all that we're alone together, talking about kissing.

She made a great effort and stumbled through her next lines. Romeo said his next line. "And then they kiss," he said. "I guess we don't need to practice that right now." He gave an embarrassed laugh.

They went on slowly through the rest of the scene. When it was over, Tamera sighed. "I stink, don't I? I'm not an actress at all. I can't do this part."

Lamar put his hands on her shoulders. "You can do it, Tamera. Don't think about the lines you've had to learn. You have to believe that you're Juliet. She's flirting with the guy. She might be Miss Innocent, but she's a great flirt. You know how to flirt, don't you?"

"Not using funny words," Tamera said, giggling nervously. She could feel the warmth of his hands on her shoulders. He was so close to her.

"You want to try it again?" he asked. "I don't have much time. I promised some friends I'd meet them at BJ's at nine."

"Oh, okay." Again Tamera felt like a pricked bubble. He wanted to get this over with as soon as possible. He wasn't interested after all.

They started the scene again. When she looked up she saw that Lamar's eyes were challenging hers. She found the words just coming out of her mouth. Suddenly she wasn't Tamera, trying hard to remember lines anymore. She was Juliet, flirting with Romeo.

The scene ended. Lamar stood there, just looking at her.

"What?" Tamera asked nervously.

"You got it, Tamera!" Lamar yelled in delight. He picked up Tamera and spun her around. "You were great."

Then he lowered her to the floor. "I guess I should be going," he said. "The guys will be wondering where I got to. But we'll do this again next week, okay?"

"Okay," Tamera said, not knowing what to think.

He had his hand on the front doorknob when he looked back. "Hey, Tamera? You want to come with me to a party at Trisha Howland's house tomorrow night?"

"Me? You're asking me to Trisha Howland's party?"

"Yeah. Want to come?"

"I'd love to," Tamera said.

"I'll pick you up around eight, then."

"Okay." Tamera knew she was beaming.

"Great." He was smiling, too. "Good night then, Juliet."

"Good night, Romeo."

The moment the door was closed, Tamera bounded up the stairs.

"That was quick," Tia said, looking up. "I guess it didn't go too well then, huh?"

"*Au contraire*, my dear sister," Tamera said, waltzing around the room. "He just invited me to Trisha's party—you know, the one that Danielle thought he was going to because she was going to be there? I can't wait to see her face when I walk through that door with Lamar. She's going to die of jealousy!"

Tamera's heart was racing as Lamar's car drew up outside a brightly lit house on Saturday night. It was still a miracle to her that she was sitting beside Lamar in his beat-up old Chevy Camaro. It was even more of a miracle that her dad had let her go. But he'd seemed to like Lamar right away. Maybe he thought the letter jacket looked trustworthy, or maybe it was the way Lamar gave him a firm handshake and called him sir.

"Just don't be too late home, and drive carefully with my little girl," was all he said as they left. In-credible! Tamera began to wonder if she was under the spell of a fairy godmother and nothing could go wrong ever again.

From inside the house came the thump of a deep

bass beat, and shadowy figures could be seen dancing behind the blinds.

"Are you sure it's okay for me to come with you?" Tamera asked in a sudden attack of nerves.

"Sure, why not?" Lamar said with a smile.

"But won't it be mainly seniors?"

"That's okay. I'll protect you," Lamar said. He put his hand on Tamera's. "Relax. It's going to be cool."

The feel of Lamar's hand, warm on her own, made Tamera forget about everything else. She walked beside him through the front door and into the crowded hallway. She had never seen so many kids crammed into one house before.

"Stay right there," Lamar said. "It's awful hot in here. I'll get us both a drink."

Tamera waited for a while, standing shyly by the wall when Danielle came out of the living room. She looked at Tamera and did a double take.

"What are you doing here?" she demanded. "Who asked you?"

Before Tamera could answer, a deep voice spoke behind Danielle. "She's with me, Danielle. I invited her."

Lamar was standing there with two cans of soda. Tamera thought she would explode with joy at the look on Danielle's face. "Fine," Danielle said, and pushed her way into the kitchen.

"You want to dance?" Lamar asked Tamera.

"I'd love to," Tamera said. At least dancing was something she could do as well as Danielle. Lamar was a great dancer, too, and Tamera was aware that other people had stopped dancing, just to watch them.

During a break in the dancing, Lamar went over to talk to some of his friends who had just come in. Tamera stood in a corner against the wall, alone and unnoticed as Maureen and one of the other senior girls came past.

"Did you see who Lamar brought with him?" the other girl asked. "I bet Danielle is having a cow."

"She's not worried," Maureen said easily. "It's pretty obvious he only brought that sophomore to make her jealous. He'll ditch the kid and take Danny home."

Tamera found it hard to breathe. Was that why Lamar had brought her to the party? Had she got it all wrong—he didn't really like her after all?

Wait a second, she told herself. I'm the one who got Juliet, not Danielle. And he was having a great time dancing with me. If she wants Lamar, she's going to have to fight for him!

Someone put on a slow dance. Couples started to sway together. Tamera took a deep breath, then went over to where Lamar was standing. "This is one of my favorite tunes, Lamar. Want to dance?" she asked.

Lamar smiled at her. "Sure. Why not?" He put his arm around her and held her close to him. She could feel his heart beating against hers. Was it possible that he was holding her like this only to make another girl jealous? Tamera didn't think so.

"I promised your dad I wouldn't keep you out too late, and I have baseball practice tomorrow," Lamar said when the dance ended. "But now I'm having too much fun to leave."

"Me, too," Tamera said.

It was close to midnight when Tamera finally went to get her coat. The party was still going strong, but Tamera didn't want to make her father mad by blowing her curfew. They were just heading for the door when Danielle appeared behind them.

"Where are you going, Lamar?" she demanded sharply.

"I'm taking Tamera home. She's feeling kind of tired," Lamar said.

"Then you're coming back, right?" Danielle asked, with a smirk on her face.

"I don't think so," Lamar said. "I'm kind of tired, too. See ya, Danny."

Tamera drifted home on a cloud of happiness. Lamar hadn't ditched her for Danielle. He really liked her.

"Tamera," he said as they drove through the darkness. "I'm really glad we're in the play together."

"Me, too," Tamera said.

"I almost didn't want to be in this play," he said. "I knew the baseball coach would give me a hard time. Just think, if I hadn't said I'd be Romeo, I'd never have gotten a chance to know you."

"You don't know how happy I was when you came through that door," Tamera said. "I thought I was stuck with Roger as Romeo."

"Now, that would have been interesting," Lamar said, laughing.

"That would have been gross," Tamera said.

Lamar pulled up outside Tamera's house. "One good thing," Lamar said. "Being Romeo and Juliet gives us a great excuse to practice. Although I don't think we really need any practice, do you?" He took Tamera's chin in his hand and kissed her gently on the lips.

"Good night, Juliet," he whispered.

Chapter 8

On Monday at school, Tamera was still floating.

"What's with you?" Sarah asked, as she grabbed her in the halls. "You've had a big grin on your face all day. I guess your private coaching session with Lamar went okay then?"

"Better than okay. How about just perfectly, wonderfully amazing?"

"What happened? Tell me all!" Sarah started shaking her.

"You won't believe this, Sarah," Tamera said. "I can hardly believe it myself. I went to Trisha's party with him."

"You did?"

"Yes, and it was incredible. He was so nice. He's the sweetest guy, Sarah. I can talk to him without worrying about saying something dumb. And I really think he likes me."

"I bet Danielle wasn't too thrilled," Sarah said.

"It was just perfect," Tamera said, smiling again as she relived the scene for the hundredth time. "You should have seen her face when she saw me with Lamar."

They walked into the cafeteria together, got their lunches, and sat down next to Tia and their other friends.

"Have you heard about Tamera?" Sarah asked.

"What about Tamera?" Marcia asked. "What have you been doing now, Tamera?"

Before Tamera could answer, Lamar walked past. He came up behind Tamera and put a hand on her shoulder. "See you later, okay?" he said, and squeezed her shoulder before he walked on.

Sarah grinned. "That," she said.

Marcia and the others were staring at Tamera as if they couldn't believe their eyes. "You and Lamar Jones?"

Tamera smiled modestly. "Romeo and Juliet have to practice together, you know."

'Wow, I wouldn't mind inviting him to my balcony," Denise said.

Tamera felt wonderful. She hoped that everyone in the cafeteria had noticed the way Lamar had put his hand on her shoulder.

That afternoon she wasn't even scared when she went to rehearsal. With Lamar there beside her, it was easy. Her lines just came to her. And when she did the scene with Lamar, her eyes never left his face. At the end of the scene, everybody applauded.

Damien came over to her. "I knew you could do it, Tamera," he said. "That was exactly what I was getting at. That was how I pictured Juliet all along. Don't change a thing, okay?"

After the rehearsal everyone came up to Tamera and told her how great she'd been. Tamera floated home that night. It had finally happened. All her wildest dreams had come true. She was a star, and she had found a great boyfriend, too. She was the luckiest girl in the world!

After that the word must have spread around school pretty quickly. Suddenly it seemed that everybody had heard of Tamera and how she was the star of the play. The very next day, some kids she didn't even know stopped her in the halls. "Are you the one who's playing Juliet?" they asked.

"That's me," Tamera said.

"Cool," one of the girls said.

"We heard you were really good," another said.

"How about that?" Tamera whispered in delight to Sarah as they moved on. "I'm famous! This is so incredible."

Even the English teacher said in the middle of class, "I've been hearing about your wonderful portrayal of Juliet, Tamera. I had no idea you were such a gifted actress."

One evening Tia came home and threw down her book bag. "Okay," she said. "Now you can be satisfied. Some guy came up to me today and asked me what it was like to be your sister. And then he said, 'Doesn't it make you feel proud?'"

Tamera grinned. "Well, doesn't it?"

"Get outta here." Tia threw her gloves at Tamera. Then she sat down beside her. "You finally did it, Tamera. You found something you were really good at. I'm very happy for you."

"Thanks, Tia," Tamera said. "Of course I suspected all along that I was destined for greatness someday. I just wasn't sure which direction I'd take. Now that I know I have acting gifts, there will be no stopping me. It probably won't make sense to go to college. I mean, why keep Hollywood waiting? And why would I need an education when I'm raking in the mega bucks."

Tia looked at her sister to see if she was joking, but Tamera's face was serious. "Tamera, you're only in one little school play," Tia said cautiously.

"Yes, but I can tell I've got what it takes. You should have seen the way the other cast members applauded when I did my scene. They love me. So does Damien. And so does Lamar, of course. He's a great guy, Tia. He tells me how wonderful I am." She jumped up. "Is that my dad's car? Great. I have to tell him that I need money right now."

"For what?" Tia asked. "Acting lessons?"

"Why would I need lessons? You've either got it or you don't. Face it, Tia, I'm a natural-born actress. When you're born with my gifts, you instinctively know what to do."

The front door opened and Ray came in.

"How's my little star?" he asked. "Any talent scouts been hammering on our door yet?"

Tia rolled her eyes.

"No, but it's only a matter of time," Tamera answered quite seriously. "And I need to talk to you, Dad. I really need to go shopping right away. I know I've had my allowance for this month, but this is an emergency."

"What kind of emergency?" Ray asked.

"I need a complete new wardrobe," Tamera said. "All my clothes are totally blah. Now that I'm a star, I have to look like a star. None of my clothes are star outfits."

Ray chuckled. "Honey, you look just fine," he said.

"Just fine when I was plain old Tamera Campbell, but now that I'm a somebody . . ."

"Aren't you taking this a little too far, Tamera?" Ray asked, not smiling now.

"Daddy, you haven't seen what it's like at school. Everybody knows who I am now. People stop me in the halls to tell me how great I am. I can't let them see me in department store clothing. It has to be all exclusive boutique designs from now on, or they'll only want to copy me and dress like me."

Ray shot Tia a worried glance.

"I'm afraid you'll just have to wait for the advance from your first movie, honey," he said. "Because I'm not giving you any money right now."

"That is so mean," Tamera complained. "I thought you wanted to help and encourage me."

"I do, but right now it sounds like you don't need

too much encouragement, Tamera," Ray said. "Your public will just have to see you looking the way you've always looked."

Tamera picked up her bag and headed upstairs. "Fine, if that's how you feel," she said stiffly.

Ray looked at Tia for help.

"It's all new to her," Tia said. "It's the first time she's been a celebrity at school. Let her enjoy it. She'll get over it—I hope."

"I hope so, too," Ray said.

Tia got up and followed Tamera upstairs. Tamera was going through her wardrobe, flinging things onto the floor. "Don't need that. Not that, it's tacky," she was saying. "Not that. Too cheap."

"Tamera, I hope you're not letting this go to your head," Tia said worriedly. "It's only a part in a play. People want to know who you are, but your fame at school is only going to last a couple of weeks. After that you'll be back to being good old Tamera again."

"Not me," Tamera said. "I get the feeling that this is the start of a beautiful new life of excitement. Leads in all the school plays, maybe drama camp in the summer, a trip out to Hollywood to meet all the producers and, who knows, signed for a sitcom before I even graduate." She looked back at Tia. "I have talent, Tia. I'm destined to be a great actress."

"Who says so?"

"Everyone. Everyone says so. I guess you're just jealous because you're not the center of attention for once."

"Not at all," Tia said. "I'm happy for you, or I was happy for you, until it started going to your head."

"It's not going to my head," Tamera said in a hurt voice. "What are you talking about? Oh, and before I forget—Lamar is coming over tonight to go through our scenes together. At least, that was what he said. Actually I'm sure it's just an excuse to be alone with me."

"Don't worry," Tia said. "I'll be upstairs, working on my boring old DNA."

"Okay, Tamera," Lamar said as he walked into the living room. "Where do you want to start?"

"Excuse me?" Tamera wasn't sure what he was getting at.

"In the play, I mean," Lamar said with a laugh. "What part of the play do you want to start with?"

"Oh, the play." Tamera laughed. "You really do want to rehearse then?"

"Of course," Lamar said. "We have to know all these lines, don't we?"

"Yeah, but we finally have a chance to be alone together, Lamar. No baseball, no rehearsal."

"I know, but we've got a lot of work to do on this play, Tamera."

"If you insist." Tamera went to her book bag and took out her script. "Let's go through the balcony scene. I love that part."

"We've got that down pretty well, I think. How about some of the other scenes." He turned the pages. "You have a lot of dialogue with the nurse. You should really rehearse with her sometime."

"With Danielle? She hates my guts."

"That doesn't matter. You both want the play to be good, don't you?"

Tamera dropped her book and wrapped her arms around Lamar's neck. "I've got a great idea. Why don't we forget about stupid rehearsing tonight and go to a movie instead?"

Lamar unwound her arms. "Tamera, get real, okay? We have to stand up in front of an audience in about four weeks' time, and we have to know an entire play. You don't want to goof up onstage, do you?"

Tamera laughed. "Don't worry," she said. "If I forget my lines when I'm up there with you, we'll just improvise, like Damien said. We can show them how Romeo and Juliet really kissed."

"You're terrible," Lamar said, laughing.

They both looked up as someone came down the stairs.

"Oh, hi," Tia said. "Don't mind me. I just need to get a snack from the kitchen."

"Hi," Lamar said. "You must be Tia."

"That's right," Tamera said for her. "And she's just leaving. She has to get back to her DNA model, don't you, Tia?" She turned to Lamar. "We act out *Romeo and Juliet* for fun. She builds models of DNA. Exciting, huh?"

"Sounds like it could be interesting," Lamar said.

"It is," Tia said, her face lighting up. "I'm doing

a project for the science fair. I'm trying to see if twins have the same DNA, and if you can see differences in their personality by the way their DNA is different."

"And can you?"

"I don't know. I haven't gotten that far yet," Tia said. "I'm still in the middle of reading all the papers and books that have been written by the experts."

Lamar looked from Tia to Tamera. "Boy, you two really are different, aren't you? I'll bet it shows up in your DNA."

"I'll let you know if it does," Tia said.

"She's not taking any of my DNA," Tamera said. "I go to sleep every night worrying that I'll wake up to find giant needles stuck in me."

"I keep telling her that one tiny cell, or a drop of saliva even, has all her DNA in it, but she's not exactly a scientific genius, you know," Tia said, smiling at Lamar.

"Shouldn't you be going back to your lab, Dr. Frankenstein?" Tamera said. "We're kind of busy here."

"Okay, I'm going," Tia said. " 'Bye, Lamar. Nice meeting you."

"Bye, Tia," Lamar said.

Tamera noticed that his eyes followed her up the stairs.

Later that night, when Lamar was gone, Tamera bounded up to their bedroom. "Listen up, sister," she said. "Lamar is my boyfriend."

"So what's your problem?" Tia asked.

"The way you were flirting with him."

"Me? Flirting? I was just making polite conversation," Tia answered.

"Oh, sure. My sister is so dumb, ha ha ha."

"I didn't say that. I was just getting even with the way you were putting me down."

"I was not putting you down," Tamera said in a shocked voice.

"Were, too. 'This is weird Tia and her boring old DNA.' That's not putting me down?"

"Okay, maybe it was," Tamera agreed. "I'm sorry. It's just that Lamar's so special and all this stuff with the play is just so amazingly wonderful. Sometimes I get scared that it might all vanish—poof! And I'll wake up and find I'm me again."

"Then just make sure you don't blow it, Tamera," Tia said.

"Why would I be stupid enough to do that?" Tamera asked. "Don't worry, sis. I think I'm getting the hang of this stardom thing just fine."

Tia rolled her eyes and went back to her reading.

Chapter 9

॰∾॰

A week later Ray came home from work to find no sign of the twins or of dinner. "Tia, Tamera, would you get down here, please?" Ray's voice echoed through the house. Tia came running down the stairs. Tamera emerged from the TV room.

"What is it, Dad?" she asked.

"I thought I told you girls that Lisa would be out tonight and that I'd need some help with dinner?" Ray said. "I have to get back to work, and I don't have much time. I thought I made that clear."

"I did the salad the way you asked," Tia said. "And I took the pork chops out of the freezer."

Ray looked at Tamera. "Someone was supposed to peel the potatoes, Tamera. And set the table?"

"Dad, do you know how many lines I have to learn by tomorrow?" Tamera said patiently. "I really don't have time for manual work right now. We don't need potatoes. They're too fattening for me anyway. Lisa said that any extra pounds show up onstage and it will be even worse when I'm on the big screen."

"You're not on the big screen yet, young lady," Ray said firmly. "And I expect you to do your share of the chores around here. Your sister is busy with her own project, but she has time to do her share."

"Miss Goody-Goody," Tamera said, giving Tia a look. "And making a model for a science fair isn't exactly as stressful as having to act the part of Juliet every day, is it? There will be thousands of people watching me when I'm onstage. They're going to expect me to be great. Now, if you'll excuse me, I'm only halfway through act three, and I have acts four and five to learn by tomorrow morning."

"Maybe you should have thought of that when you went out with Lamar last night," Ray said.

"I need some fun, you know," Tamera said. "And Lamar and I need time alone together. Most of the time we're just working on the play."

"I still can't believe that Lamar took you to the Fleur-de-Lys," Tia said.

"I don't see why not," Tamera said.

"But that place is so expensive, Tamera. Does Lamar really have that kind of money?"

"It was a special celebration because we've been together for three weeks now," Tamera said. "And anyway, it's good for me to get used to being seen in the right places. I have to feel at home in expensive restaurants. My public will expect it from me when I'm in Hollywood."

"Tamera, you're talking a lot of nonsense tonight," Ray said. "You're in a school play, that's all. Enough of this talking big. In this house you're just one of the family, and I expect you to do your chores. Now, set that table before I get really angry."

"You'll be sorry," Tamera said in a clipped voice. She started banging knives and forks down into the table. Ray gave Tia a worried look.

As the rehearsals went on and the performance date got closer, Tia began to feel more and more worried about Tamera. Tamera wasn't acting like herself at all. Usually she hated snobby, obnoxious people, and now she had turned into one. It was as if she were possessed and she couldn't stop being an actress for one second.

"Where's Tamera?" Tia asked as she joined Sarah and their other friends in the lunch line.

"You mean Detroit's answer to Robin Givens, Vanessa Williams, and Whitney Houston all rolled into one?" Sarah said.

"She's behaving like that at rehearsals?" Tia asked.

"You'd better believe it," Sarah said. "She's acting like a big pain, Tia. In fact she's—" She broke off as Tamera eased herself into the line beside them.

"Hey, no cuts," a boy in line called out.

Tamera gave him a withering stare. "Do you know who I am?" she said coldly. "I only have fifteen minutes to eat before I have to be at a special rehearsal for the play."

The line moved on. Tia ordered a slice of pizza and a banana. Tamera stared at the menu.

"Hurry up, honey," the lunch lady said impatiently. "We've got a whole long line waiting."

"You don't have any salads on the menu," Tamera said. "Couldn't you make me a special order of cottage cheese and a simple green salad?"

"We don't do special orders," the woman said.

"I thought you might make an exception for me," Tamera said. "Seeing that it's so important I look good onstage. I can get you free tickets to my opening night."

"Oh, are you a rock singer or something?" The woman's face lit up.

"No, I'm in the school play. *Romeo and Juliet,*" Tamera said. "I play Juliet."

"Thanks, but you'd have to pay me to go to Shakespeare." The woman chuckled. "Now, do you want the pizza or the burger or the turkey sandwich?"

Tamera snatched the turkey sandwich and stalked across the cafeteria. "Rude person," she said. "But I guess women who work in cafeterias can't be expected to appreciate culture." She looked around in disgust. "There's nowhere to sit," she said. She went over to a table of freshmen girls. "Sorry, but you'll have to move," she said.

"What for?" The girls looked up nervously.

"Because I only have a few minutes to eat and I need to sit somewhere," Tamera said. "I'm Tamera Campbell, in case you don't recognize me. You know—star of the play? Now, beat it."

"Tamera," Tia said in horror, digging her sister in the ribs. "You can't just talk to people like that. There's a table over there now. Stop acting like a jerk."

"If I were a little freshman, I'd be honored to give up my seat to me," Tamera said. "The young have no respect these days."

She sat down next to Tia and Denise. "Okay," she said. "'Which of you is coming shopping with me on Saturday? I need a dress to wear to the opening night party."

"I'll come if you like," Marcia said.

"No, Marcia, not you. I need someone with good taste," Tamera said.

"Tamera!" Tia exclaimed. "That is so rude. You can't talk to your friends like that or you'll soon wind up with no friends."

"What are you making a fuss about, Tia? Marcia understands that my time is very precious right now. I need someone who can help me choose a great dress in ten minutes flat. You'd probably be the best person, Sarah. Saturday, ten-thirty at the mall. Be there."

"I'm sorry, Tamera, but I'm busy on Saturday," Sarah said.

"So am I," Denise added.

Tamera's lips clenched together. "I think you're all being very selfish when it's so important for me to look good," she said, getting up. "Now I don't have time to eat lunch. One of you can have this," she said, pushing her turkey sandwich down the table before she left.

"You see how bad it's getting?" Sarah said to Tia. "I don't know what's gotten into her. She used to be such a fun person. Now I'm really sorry I talked her into going to tryouts with me. Can't you say something to her?"

"I've tried, believe me," Tia said. "I just wish I knew what to do, Sarah. Every time I talk to her, she gives me this spiel about how it's tough being a star and how everyone has to make allowances for great artists."

"Give me a break," Sarah said. "She's not even that good. She's always screwing up her lines, because she hasn't taken the trouble to learn them properly. I can tell that Damien is getting really fed up with her. I wish you would talk to her, Tia, before it's too late and she really blows it."

Tia couldn't concentrate at school because she was worrying about Tamera. She thought of talking to her mom or Tamera's dad, but she didn't want to get Tamera in trouble. She knew that Tamera's dad would be really mad if he knew how Tamera had been acting at school. Then the answer dawned on her—she'd try to get a chance to talk to Lamar. If anyone could get through to Tamera, he could.

She found out where his locker was and got to school early the next morning. She was going over in her head exactly what she should say to him when he came in through the big double doors. Lamar's face lit up when he saw her. "Tia," he said, "I've been hoping I'd run into you. I thought of calling you at home, but then I was scared that Tamera might pick up the phone."

"I was hanging around your locker, hoping to bump into you," Tia confessed.

"You were? Then I guess we're both having the same problem right now."

"'Tamera?" Tia asked.

"You got it," Lamar said. "I really liked her, Tia. I thought she was the neatest girl I'd ever met. She was so excited about things, and she was such fun to be with. But now she's turned into this different person. It's scary."

"She acts that way with you, too?" Tia said. "She's crazy about you, Lamar. I thought at least she'd be nice to you."

"Oh, she's nice enough to me," Lamar said, "but it's embarrassing being around her, Tia. At that fancy restaurant the other night, she was so rude to the waitress, and she made a big fool of herself, ordering stuff when she didn't know what it was. And she's even worse at rehearsals now. She thinks she knows better than everyone. She's always stopping Damien to make suggestions and telling everyone how to say their lines."

"She's never done anything this big before," Tia said. "I guess it's gone to her head."

"Then I hope it goes out of her head again before it's too late," Lamar said. "She's not easy to be around right now."

"Tell me about it," Tia said. "You don't have to live with her, Lamar. I'm trying to be understanding, but one day soon I'm going to blow my top."

"Can't you talk to her, Tia?"

"I thought maybe you could say something, Lamar," Tia said. "If she'd listen to anyone right now, it would have to be you. And if she thought she'd lost you as a friend, then maybe she'd wise up."

"I could try," Lamar said. "But I don't think it's going to be easy. I think she's living in this fantasy world right now where she really believes she's a star. It's going to take something pretty big to burst her bubble."

He stopped talking and looked up as Tamera came down the hall toward them.

"Oh, so that's where you got to, Tia," she said. "I was looking all over for you." Her gaze went from Tia to Lamar. "What are you doing?" she asked suspiciously.

"I just bumped into Lamar and we were talking," Tia said.

"I'd prefer it if you didn't talk to my boyfriend around school," Tamera said. "I don't want people getting the wrong idea. Lamar, you didn't call me last night. What happened?"

"I was . . . uh . . . kind of busy," he said. "We won't be using scripts from today on, remember. I had to make sure I knew all my lines."

Tamera patted his shoulder. "Lamar, honey, you worry too much. You should learn to believe in yourself, like I do. Tell yourself you are a great actor and the play is lucky to have you. It works for me." She broke off as the bell rang. "Oh, well, there's the first bell. Gotta run. See you at rehearsal. 'Bye!"

"Like I said," Lamar commented, looking after her. "I'll try talking to her tonight, but it's not going to be easy."

At the beginning of rehearsal, Tamera went straight up to Damien.

"Can I talk to you, please?" she said.

Damien looked up from the conversation he was having with other cast members.

"What is it now, Tamera?" he asked. "You've re-written the whole fifth act so that Juliet doesn't die?"

"That is so funny," Tamera said. "Good idea, though. No, I wanted to talk to you about my costume. I saw the blue dress that the wardrobe people picked out for me, and frankly it's not me at all. So I've come up with my own design, and I thought I'd get Tia's mother to make it. She's a fashion designer, you know. I see myself in hot pink and orange, very slinky and sort of swirling out at the floor."

"Tamera, we're using the costume from the wardrobe, and it's going to be blue," Damien said.

"But blue isn't really my color, Damien," Tamera said. "I'm more a fun color kind of person."

Damien was trying hard to keep his cool. "I see Juliet in blue and white," he said, "and we don't have the money to get new costumes for every play, so I'm afraid you're stuck with it, Tamera. So no more costume suggestions, okay? We have a zillion things to get through today, and I can't take any more interruptions." He clapped his hands. "All right, places for a complete run-through. No books, Tamera."

Reluctantly Tamera put down her script. The run-through began. Only three minutes had passed when Tamera held up her hand. "Hold on a second, I've got a brilliant idea," she said. "How would it be if Romeo came through the audience the first time we see him, not in through that archway? That is so ordinary. Or, wait a second, it's coming to me—he swings down on a rope!"

Damien ran his hands nervously through his hair. "Tamera, we're not doing Tarzan, and we're not changing things around now. We only have two weeks to get everything perfect. Get on with it."

Tamera's scene with the nurse and her mother started.

Damien held up a hand to stop them. "Tamera, for pete's sake would you say what's written for once! You said, 'It's an honor I've never dreamed about.' The real line is 'It's an honor I dream not of.' "

"I was always told it was wrong to finish a sentence with a preposition," Tamera said. "Besides, that was close enough."

"We don't mess with Shakespeare," Damien yelled. "He was only the greatest writer ever in the English language. If he wants to finish with a preposition, then he can!"

"You don't have to yell," Tamera said.

"Just get on with it, Tamera. You're holding everyone up."

Tamera continued speaking, then walked across the stage, crossing in front of Danielle.

"Wait a second," Danielle interrupted. "Why is she over there?" She glared at Tamera. "You're not keeping to your blocking. You were supposed to stand center stage while I finish my speech."

"I just felt like walking in front of you today," Tamera said.

"But that's not what we blocked," Danielle snapped. "You put it in your script, didn't you?"

Tamera gave her a pitying look. "Danielle, a great actress can't be tied down by little marks in a book. She has to do what she feels is right at the moment. And today I feel like crossing the stage and standing over here."

Danielle put her hands on her hips and turned to Damien. "This is hopeless," she said. "How am I expected to say my lines if I don't know where I should be facing?"

"Improvise, honey," Tamera said. "It might make your speeches less boring."

"Boring? Me? At least I get my lines right. I give other people the right cues. The rest of us just have to wait and guess when you've finished because you never say the same thing twice."

"Boy, do you have some nerve, talking to me like that," Tamera said in an icy voice. She strode over to Damien. "I've had enough of her insults. She's been jealous of me all along and she's done nothing but bug me ever since day one. Well, I'm not going to put up with it any longer. I want her kicked out of the play right now, Damien. Get rid of her!"

Damien got up from his stool. "Thank you, Tamera," he said. "You've helped me make up my mind to do something really difficult."

"You're going to kick her out? Good for you," Tamera said.

Damien shook his head. "No, I'm not going to get rid of Danielle, Tamera. I'm getting rid of you."

Chapter 10

*T*here was a horrified silence. Then a voice muttered, "All right!" and there was some applause.

"Excuse me?" Tamera demanded. "I don't think I heard right."

"Then I'll say it more clearly," Damien said. "You're fired, Tamera. You're out of here. Goodbye."

"You're firing me? Are you crazy?" Tamera shrieked. "I am the best thing that's ever happened to the Roosevelt High Drama club."

"I thought so too when we picked you," Damien said, "but you've been nothing but trouble ever since. I can't take it anymore. You're upsetting the entire cast, and you're spoiling the whole show."

"Fine," Tamera said, gathering up her things as she spoke. "Try to get along without me. You'll be sorry. Who do you think you'll get to play Juliet in my place?"

"We have an understudy," Damien said. "And she'll do just fine. Nobody could be as much of a pain as you're being."

Tamera clutched her book bag to her. "I give you two days," she said. "That will be how long it takes before you beg me to come back." She gave Damien a pitying look. "Your problem, Damien, is that you don't appreciate an artistic temperament. You've only worked with ordinary high school actors before. And frankly, you don't have the imagination to make a boring old Shakespeare play fun. The audience will all be asleep before the end of the first act. And if you want to know, I'm glad to be out of it."

She swept out of the door in a dramatic exit.

"Dumb, stupid, idiotic, boring, narrow-minded . . ." she muttered to herself as she stomped down the hall. But she found that her legs were shaking and she could hardly hold the books she clutched in her arms. Deep inside her she knew that she had just blown it—her big chance to be somebody. She couldn't believe what she had just done. But she wouldn't let herself stop to think.

"Two days," she kept on muttering. "That's what it will take before they decide they can't live without me. Then I'm not even sure I'll go back. Boy, are they going to be sorry!"

Then she swallowed hard, because a lump kept creeping up into her throat and she was terrified she might cry in public. She ran all the way home from the bus. She had to tell Tia. Tia would understand.

Tia would be on her side. Tia would believe that that witch Danielle had been out to get her and it was all her fault.

"Tia? Where are you?" Tamera yelled. She ran up the stairs. Their bedroom was empty, with only one giant model of a DNA strand standing between the two beds.

"How mean can you get?" Tamera said out loud. "She's always here working at that stupid DNA, but when I really need her, she's nowhere around."

She sat on her bed and pressed her lips together hard, willing herself not to cry.

"Boy, am I glad to be out of that craziness," she said to the empty room. "Those rehearsals were pathetic. Nobody knew what they were doing, everyone was so bad. The play's going to be a big flop. And now I have all this time to myself. I can go shopping. I can hang out at the cafe at the mall with my friends and see all the movies I've missed. Yeah, life's back to normal. I wasn't meant to do all this hard work. When I'm a movie star, I'll only shoot when I feel like it, and there will be no long, boring rehearsals, and I'll make up my own words. It's going to be great." She jumped up from the bed. "And you know what else?" she asked herself. "I can watch *Oprah* again. Yeah!"

She ran downstairs and got herself a couple of Twinkies and a bowl of ice cream. Then she switched on the TV, with the volume up very loud, as if she needed enough noise to stop herself from thinking.

*   *   *

98

After school Tia was about to head for home when she passed the auditorium. She stood for a while, looking at the doors and listening to raised voices echoing from the stage. She was very curious to see for herself just how much of a pain Tamera was being. If she really was bad enough, then she had decided to talk to her mom about it that night. She opened the door silently and crept into the auditorium.

There were a lot of people onstage, and something close to chaos was going on.

"I just can't do this," a girl was saying, and she was crying.

Lamar had his arm around her. "Just give it a try, Janine," he was saying to her.

Tia looked around in surprise. There was no sign of Tamera. Tia went forward cautiously. Suddenly people onstage were aware of her. They fell silent, one by one until they were all looking at her. Tia stopped, feeling very embarrassed.

"Why have you come back?" Danielle demanded. "You went home to change your clothes and thought that would make a difference, or what?"

"Excuse me," Tia said, clearing her throat nervously. "I just wondered where my sister was."

"Your sister?" Damien asked.

"That's Tia, Tamera's twin sister," Lamar said. "Hi, Tia. I'm afraid you're too late for the big scene."

"What big scene?"

Lamar came to the edge of the stage. "Damien just fired Tamera. She walked out, very mad."

"Oh no," Tia said. "That's just terrible. I feel so bad for her. But I guess she had it coming, didn't she?"

"She was impossible," Damien said, coming over to join Lamar. He was looking at Tia with interest. "You're Tamera's twin? That's incredible. You look exactly alike. You even sound exactly alike."

He leaped down from the stage to stand beside Tia. "Are you exactly alike in other things, too? In personality, maybe?"

Tia laughed. "Not at all. I study hard, for one thing. Grades are important to me. I'm very responsible. Tamera's a bit of a goof-off. And I'm kind of shy, compared to Tamera."

Damien put an arm around her shoulder. "Tell me, Tia, have you ever thought of acting in a play? We're desperate for a Juliet right now. We thought we had an understudy, but she's home with laryngitis and we don't know when she'll be able to rehearse. If you're really smart, maybe you could learn lines in a hurry. The play's in two weeks."

"I don't know . . . Tia began. "I am kind of busy right now. I have a science fair project I have to complete pretty soon."

"We'd make it as easy for you as possible. We'd arrange rehearsals around your schedule if you like. I'm sure Lamar would work with you," Damien pleaded.

"I don't think so," Tia said. "It wouldn't be fair to my sister, would it?"

"Tia, if you really want to help your sister, then

take the part," Damien said. "She needs teaching a lesson. She was doing great as Juliet until it went to her head. Then she turned into the world's biggest prima donna. I thought that firing her might wake her up and make her realize that she wasn't as great as she thought she was and that we would do just fine without her, but I don't think it has. She walked out telling us we'd be sorry."

Lamar touched Tia's arm. "Maybe if she finds out you're taking her part, it might shock her into realizing what she's done."

"And it might make her decide that she hates my guts," Tia said. "I have to live with her, you know."

"I know, and I guess it won't be easy," Damien said. "She's not exactly Miss Congeniality right now, is she? But I get the feeling she won't be too much fun to be around whether you take the part or not."

Tia nodded. "You might be right there," she said. "And Tamera does need a wake-up call." She stared across the stage, then she nodded. "Okay, I'll do it," she said. "Show me what I have to do."

It was past six when Tia finally got home. Lisa was out, manning her fashion cart at the mall, and Ray hadn't returned from work. Tamera was on her fifth Twinkie and was feeling sick and angry by the time Tia walked in the door.

"Where have you been?" Tamera demanded. "The only time I need someone to talk to, you're not around."

"Sorry," Tia said, "but I had something important to do."

"Like what? More talks with DNA geeks? More boring research in the library?"

"No, Tamera," Tia said. "I was busy trying to learn your part in the play."

"Excuse me?" Tamera demanded.

"I agreed to take over your part in the play," Tia said again. "I'm going to be Juliet instead of you."

Tamera put her hand to her mouth as if she were trying to stop herself from bursting out laughing. "You? That is so funny. Boy, they must be desperate. I guess they just needed someone to fit the costume."

"What makes you think I was so bad?" Tia asked.

Tamera was still convulsed in phony giggles.

"When did you ever do any acting?"

"You didn't either until this," Tia said.

"But I have talent," Tamera said. "It was obvious from day one that I was an actress. You're so shy they probably can't even hear what you're saying."

"Damien seemed to think I did pretty well for the first time," Tia said.

"Right. He was probably just trying to be nice." Then a big smile spread across her face. "Oh, I get it! He wants to make me so mad that I'll beg him to have my part back. He knew right away that he'd made a big mistake when he fired me, but he didn't know how to stop me when I walked out. This is so funny."

"I don't think it's funny at all, Tamera," Tia said.

"In fact I think it's pretty sad. You lost your big chance to be in a play. What's funny about that?"

"The play was going to be a disaster anyway," Tamera said. "That Damien guy doesn't have a clue about directing. He couldn't take suggestions. He wouldn't let me do what I felt was right. It was turning into a big pain."

"I heard there was only one big pain and that was you," Tia said.

"Me? I was just trying to help save the play," Tamera said. "I was the only one there with artistic talent. But they didn't want to hear what I had to say. Fine. Let them make fools of themselves. And you can make a fool of yourself, too. Although I'm surprised you took the part. I thought you were so super busy with your DNA that you couldn't help me with my lines."

"I *am* super busy," Tia said. "And I don't really have any time. But if you really want to know, Tamera, I was so embarrassed by the way you behaved that I thought I should try and make up for you. I didn't want them to think that both of us had big egos."

"I don't have a big ego," Tamera said.

"Oh no—only one the size of Alaska," Tia said. "Everyone has been saying so."

"So you believe everyone else, huh? Some sister you turned out to be," Tamera said. "Okay, go ahead with your dumb play. Personally, I'm glad to be out of it. No more stressful rehearsals. From now on I just get to enjoy myself. And don't come to me if you want help with the lines either."

"I won't need to, thanks," Tia said. "Both Damien and Lamar have offered to work with me."

Tamera's eyes narrowed. "Let's get one thing clear, Tia," she said. "You can take my part in the play, but start messing with my boyfriend and you'll be sorry!"

Later that evening Tia went down to supper.

"Where's Tamera?" Lisa asked. "Didn't she hear me calling?"

"She's not coming," Tia said. She looked from her mother's face to Ray's. There was no way she could tell him that Tamera had lost her part in the play and she had agreed to do it instead. Ray might know that Tamera had been acting like a prima donna recently, but she was still his little girl, his princess. And Tia didn't think he'd understand that she'd taken the part to help Tamera, not to spite her. And anyway, Tia decided, that was something Tamera was going to have to tell him herself.

"She's, uh, not hungry tonight," Tia added as she sat down.

"Don't tell me she's still on this dieting kick!" Lisa exclaimed. "I wish I'd never told her that the stage adds pounds to your appearance. I hope she's not getting anorexic or anything."

"She's fine, Mom," Tia said. "She's just a little strung out right now and she's not in the mood to talk. Besides, she was on her fifth Twinkie when I got home, if that makes you feel any better."

"Smart girl," Lisa said with a chuckle. "Twinkies are the best diet food I know."

"I hope she's not working too hard on this play," Ray said. "It means a whole lot to her, doesn't it? And it's the first time in her life that she's done anything this important. I just hope it's not too much of a strain on her. Do you think she's handling it okay, Tia?"

Tia felt sick inside. She felt so bad for Tamera, even though she knew it was all Tamera's fault. "I guess," she said.

Chapter 11

❀❀

When Tamera woke up in the morning, she felt as if her insides had tied themselves into big knots. For a second she couldn't remember why, then it all came back to her. She had to go to school and face everybody. All those faces looking at her and knowing that Damien had kicked her out of the play. She wouldn't be Tamera the star anymore. She'd be Tamera the nobody, the one who couldn't keep her part in the play. Worse still, she'd be Tia's sister again.

What do I care what they think? she told herself. When they see how bad the play is and how Tia stinks as Juliet, then they'll all know why I got out.

She made sure she got to school just as the bell for first period was ringing and the hallways were already empty. She went from class to class with her head held high and an expression on her face that said clearly, Don't talk to me.

At lunchtime she joined her friends in the cafeteria. She could tell from the way they were looking at her that they had just been talking about her, but she was going to put them straight right away.

"Okay," she said, sitting down next to Denise and turning on her brightest smile. "Who's coming to the mall this afternoon? Cafe Piccolo—my treat?"

"Sorry, Tamera," Denise said. "I've signed up to help with scenery for the play."

"Marcia? Chantal? Michelle?" Tamera looked down the table.

"Sorry, Tamera. We're helping, too," Marcia said.

"I don't know why you guys are wasting your time on that play," Tamera said with a phony laugh. "It's going to be so bad. I can't tell you how glad I am to be out of it. I was looking for a way to quit. And poor Tia, she's just going to end up making a fool of herself."

"Actually, Tia was pretty good last night," Sarah said. "I was impressed. And Damien couldn't believe how well she could read all those hard lines."

"That's pretty obvious, isn't it," Tamera said. "She'd heard me reading them over and over at home. They were already there in her subconscious. But the big question is—can she act?"

"She sounded good, Tamera," Sarah said. "Even Danielle told her that she was . . ." She paused and shook her head. "Never mind," she said. "But you don't have to worry about Tia. She'll do just great."

"Well, isn't that special," Tamera said. She didn't say anything more about the play. But the sick, sinking feeling in her stomach wouldn't go away. They weren't missing her at all. Tia was going to be great as Juliet, and nobody would notice Tamera again. She knew now how stupid she had been, but she wasn't going to admit it, even to herself.

Why didn't somebody stop me? she asked herself angrily. But deep down she knew that Tia had tried to warn her, and so had her friends and Lamar.

When she thought about Lamar, her heart started thumping with worry. When would she ever get to see him? What if he didn't like her anymore, now that she wasn't in the play? She had to know.

After lunch she went looking for Lamar and found him in the school yard, shooting hoops with a bunch of guys.

"Hey, Lamar," she called brightly. There was no way he was going to see how upset she was.

He came over to her. "Hi, Tamera."

"You didn't call me last night," Tamera said.

"I, uh, didn't know what to say, Tamera," Lamar said. "I was pretty upset by that scene yesterday."

"Me, too," Tamera said. "I never believed that creep Damien would be stupid enough to get rid of the one person who could act—except you, of course. I feel really bad about it now."

"You do?" Lamar looked hopeful.

"Yes, because I left you to work with a bunch of losers. I really think that you should quit, too. It will only make you look bad if you stay."

"I don't want to quit, Tamera," Lamar said. "I like being in the play. I really liked being in the play with you, but I guess that's not an option anymore."

"No, it's not. Instead you've got yourself stuck with my sister, who might be the world's smartest person, but who hasn't got a clue abut acting."

"I thought Tia did okay yesterday," Lamar said. "You'd have been proud of her. I thought it was great of her to agree to help out like that when she's already so busy."

"Oh yeah, that's my sister, the saint," Tamera said. "Good old Tia. She's always there to help out."

Lamar looked around uncomfortably. "I should be getting back to the guys," he said.

"So, how about getting together after your play rehearsal tonight?" Tamera asked. "We could go out for pizza."

Lamar shook his head. "I really can't, Tamera," he said. "I'm up to my eyes in work right now. It's just crazy, what with the play and my baseball coach mad at me because I skipped a practice."

"But you will call me, won't you?" Tamera asked.

"If I have time," Lamar said.

"Okay," Tamera said quietly.

"I have to get back," Lamar said, and started heading back to the group of guys. Tamera watched him, wanting to say something but not knowing what to say. She felt as if she were riding a roller coaster, going faster and faster, down and down, out of control, and there was no way of stopping it.

*   *   *

After school that afternoon Tamera went alone to the mall.

"Shopping therapy," she said to herself. "That's what I need." But nothing made her feel better. She tried on a couple of outfits, and they both looked ugly. She listened to new CDs and didn't like any of them. When she sat down at last and ordered herself a double latte with whipped cream and cinnamon on top, it tasted bitter, and she didn't even finish it.

I don't know what's the matter with me, she thought. I don't even want to hang around the mall anymore. But she didn't want to go home either. She hadn't yet told her dad or Lisa that she had quit the play. And she was sure that Tia hadn't told them that she had taken over Tamera's role. Now she realized that she didn't want to face her dad. He'd give her a lecture about showing off and getting a swelled head. He'd be wrong, of course, but she didn't want to hear it all the same.

So she kept on walking, aimlessly, from store to store, stopping to look in windows that didn't even interest her. She made sure she didn't go anywhere near Lisa's fashion cart, just in case Lisa was there and saw her. It was still too early to go home, but she couldn't stand the music or the crowds any longer. She left the mall and started to walk home, taking a shortcut across the park. The cold wind in her face made her feel better and she strode out, swinging her arms.

"Nothing can stop Tamera Campbell," she said out

loud. "She's going right to the top, and then all those creeps are going to be sorry they were mean to me."

Suddenly she froze, shrinking back into the shade of a big tree. A car was parked beside the duck pond. She recognized it right away. It was Lamar's car. He was sitting in it, and Tia was sitting beside him. Lamar had his arm along the back of the seat, behind Tia, and their heads were close together.

It's okay, Tamera told herself. They're just rehearsing. Lamar said he'd give her extra help.

But as she watched them, she could tell they weren't reading from a script. They were talking. Lamar reached out and touched Tia's arm. Tia looked up at Lamar and smiled. Tamera felt the anger growing inside her like a balloon. She wanted to run over to that car and drag them both out and let them know what she thought of them.

But there were little kids and old people walking past and she didn't want to make a scene in front of other people. Besides, it wasn't Lamar's fault if Tia was flirting with him, was it? She'd hurry home and wait for Tia there. And when Tia got home, she was going to get it.

All the way home Tamera got madder and madder, until she was ready to burst. How dare Tia do that to her! First she stole her part in the play, and now she was trying to steal her boyfriend. She stood by the window, waiting for Lamar's car to drive up.

"So, what are we going to do, Tia?" Lamar asked as he turned into Tia's street.

Tia sighed. "I just wish I knew, Lamar. We both want to help her, but it's not working, is it? It's pretty obvious neither of us is getting through to her. If getting kicked out of the play didn't wake her up, I don't know what will."

"I think I'm just going to have to tell her that I don't want to see her again," Lamar said. "I just can't handle her like this, Tia. I'm embarrassed to be with her. She's blaming everyone else except herself."

"I know, and it's just not like her," Tia said. "She's a great person, Lamar. Okay, so she's always been a goof-off, but she's fun and she's not usually selfish either. She risked her own life to rescue me from a fire once. She gave up going to Disney World to come down to Texas and get me out of a bad situation there. She's changed completely. I don't even know her."

"I don't want to know her like this," Lamar said. He stopped the car outside Tia's house. "Thanks for being such a great listener, Tia," he said. "If one good thing has come out of it, it's that you and I have gotten to be good friends."

Tia smiled at him. "We're fellow sufferers," she said.

"If you come up with any brilliant suggestions, let me know, okay? Otherwise I'm just going to call her up and tell her it's over."

"Poor Tamera," Tia said. "I know she's behaved badly to everyone, but I can't help feeling sorry for her. She had her one big chance and she's spoiled everything."

"We did our best, Tia," Lamar said. "It's not our problem if she won't wise up. I feel bad, too, because I really liked her."

He leaned across to Tia. "Thanks for being there, Tia," he said. "See you at rehearsal, okay?" He gave her a little kiss on her forehead. Tia got out of the car and ran up the front path.

"Welcome home, traitor," said a voice in her ear as she closed the front door behind her.

"Tamera, you scared me," Tia said, spinning around. Tamera was standing there with her hands on her hips, her eyes blazing.

"I was waiting for you to get home, Tia," Tamera said. "Where were you?"

"Lamar drove me home," Tia said. "We were just having a little talk."

"Sure you were," Tamera said. "You can't fool me, Tia Landry. I saw you, sitting together in the park. I saw his arm around you. I saw you gazing up into his eyes and smiling at him. Traitor!"

"Tamera, it wasn't like that at all," Tia said. She took off her jacket and started up the stairs.

"I warned you, Tia," Tamera said, following one step behind. "I told you to stay away from my boyfriend. But no—you have to take everything away from me, don't you?"

"I didn't take anything away from you," Tia said.

"Oh no? My part in the play? My glory? And now my boyfriend?"

"You gave it all away yourself, Tamera," Tia said.

She pushed open the bedroom door. "You acted like a jerk until nobody could stand you any longer."

"Boy, have you got a nerve," Tamera yelled. "You couldn't stand it when I had the limelight for once, could you? You didn't like me being the star at school. Some sister you turned out to be, Tia Landry. I wish I'd never bumped into you in that store. I wish I'd never known you existed."

"Tamera, everything I did was for your own good," Tia tried to explain.

"Oh, sure it was. Trying to steal my boyfriend? Nice, Tia. Real sweet of you."

"I wasn't trying to steal your boyfriend, I was just—" Tia tried to say, but Tamera wasn't listening.

"Ever since you came here, I've always had to play second fiddle to you," she screamed. "I let you come live in my house, I even share my room with you, and what happens? You always have to be the important one. You have to win the contests. You have to get the praise and make the honor roll. I can't even walk around in my own room, with your stupid DNA model taking up all the space. I don't have anything of my own anymore, thanks to you."

"Fine, if that's how you feel," Tia said, fighting to keep calm. "If you don't want me here, I'll ask my mom if we can move out again." She went to the closet and started taking out clothes.

"What are you doing?" Tamera demanded.

"Pretty obvious, isn't it?" Tia said. "I'm moving my clothes out of your room. I'll store them in my mom's room until we can find another place to go."

Tamera felt as if she were drowning in deep water. I don't want you to go, she wanted to yell. Don't leave me, Tia. But Tia calmly went on taking armfuls of clothes out of the closet.

"Stop, don't be stupid!" Tamera yelled, grabbing hold of Tia's arm.

"Let go of me," Tia shouted. "Just get out of my way, okay? I'm doing what you want. I'm getting out of your life. You'll never have to see me again."

"Put that stuff back," Tamera commanded. She wrestled with Tia's arm.

"Stop it!" Tia screamed. "Let go of me." She broke free of Tamera and headed for the bedroom door, her arms full of clothes.

Tamera grabbed her and dragged her back. One of the hangers Tia was carrying snagged on the bedspread. Without warning Tia lost her balance and fell into Tamera. They both toppled over and crashed into the giant DNA model. It fell to the ground and broke into a hundred tiny pieces.

Chapter 12

❀

*F*or a long moment neither of them moved, lying there with the breath knocked out of them, too stunned to get up.

Then Tia scrambled to her feet, took a long look at her destroyed model, and let out a despairing wail. "My model! My beautiful model! Do you know how long it took me to build it? And now it's ruined. I'll never be able to make it again in time for the science fair. Now I'll never win a prize. I'll never get to a good college some day."

She threw herself down on her bed, and her body shook with deep, terrible sobs.

Tamera got to her feet cautiously. She stood there looking at Tia, feeling as if her own heart were breaking. It hurt her more than she could imagine to see Tia that way. She knew what it was like to have your dreams crushed in one terrible second. But in her case, it had been all her own fault. She had deserved to be kicked out of the play. But it wasn't Tia's fault that the model was broken. Tamera realized that she cared about Tia more than anything else in the world. She would do anything she could to make things right again.

She sat down beside Tia and put a cautious hand on Tia's back. "Please don't cry, Tia," she said. "I'm so sorry. I'm really, really sorry for everything. It's all my fault. Please don't cry. I'll help you build it again."

"Do you know how much work I put into that?" Tia gasped between sobs.

"We can do it again. I'll help," Tamera said. "It won't take long. Look." She knelt on the ground and started stacking blocks, one on top of the other. "Look, Tia—the blocks still fit on top of each other, it's already half-built again. We'll get it done in time for the science fair."

Tia raised her tearstained face as Tamera continued to work feverishly, stacking blocks. "You don't understand, Tamera," she said. "All of the blocks were in order. They had to match the DNA sequence I was writing about in my paper. The person with DNA like you're making would either be dead or have two heads or something."

"But the colors look prettier my way," Tamera said. "I never did like orange next to yellow." She looked up from her block building and caught Tia's eye. Tia's lower lip began to twitch, and she started to laugh. "Tamera, you're something else," she said. Tamera started laughing, too. They looked at each other and fell into each other's arms in a giant hug, laughing and crying at the same time.

"Oh, Tia, I've been so dumb. Please say you'll forgive me," Tamera begged.

"Of course I forgive you. I'm just glad something finally got through to you. You were acting so weird, Tamera. I was really scared."

"Me, too," Tamera said. "I was scared of me. It was like I was on this roller coaster to destruction, and I couldn't stop it. You finally stopped it for me, Tia. When I saw you crying, I knew that you mattered to me more than anything else. It really broke my heart when I thought I'd spoiled your big chance."

"That is so sweet, Tamera," Tia said, gazing at her fondly. "I'm sure we'll be able to fix it in time."

"I still think you should leave it like this," Tamera said, looking at the brightly colored tower of blocks.

"It would certainly blow their minds at the science fair." Tia laughed.

"That's probably my DNA," Tamera said, laughing, too. "Crazy and mixed up. I bet all the good parts went to you. I ended up with the orange and yellow bits."

Tia put her arm around Tamera's shoulder. "Don't talk that way, Tamera. There are lots of good parts to you."

"Like what?" Tamera said. "I'm not smart like you,

and I'm not even a nice person. I totally blew my one chance to be a somebody."

"You let it go to your head," Tia said.

"I know," Tamera agreed. "I don't know what got into me, Tia. I could hear myself saying all these horrible things and acting so stupidly, but I couldn't stop myself. It was like I was possessed by an evil twin."

"Cut that out right now," Tia said, wagging a finger at Tamera. "We already have enough twins around here, without adding an evil one."

"But it was so dumb of me, Tia," Tamera said. "I wanted so much to be a success in the play. I wanted to be the kind of person other people admired, and I ended up with everyone hating me."

"You know why, Tamera?" Tia said gently. "Really great people never throw their weight around. They never act like superstars. It's only the wannabes who try to make themselves think they're important."

"I know that now," Tamera said. "But it's too late, isn't it? I've blown all my chances. I'm not in the play anymore, and Lamar likes you better than me."

"But, Tamera—" Tia began, but Tamera held up her hand.

"It's okay. I can understand why," Tamera said. "You're a nicer person than me. I was pretty horrible to be around."

"Tamera, you've got it all wrong," Tia said. "Lamar doesn't like me better than you."

"But I saw you together. You were smiling at each other. He had his arm around you."

"We were talking about you," Tia said. "Lamar was really worried about you and so was I. We stopped on the way home to see if we could come up with a way to help you. We wanted to stop you before it was too late."

"Lamar still likes me?" Tamera asked hesitantly.

"He wants to," Tia said. "He just didn't like the way you were behaving. He felt really bad that you'd been kicked out of the play."

"He's not the only one," Tamera said. "I feel so terrible about it. Now I'll have to come to the play and watch you being great as Juliet. And I'll have to hear everyone telling me how talented and smart my sister is again."

Tia looked fondly at her sister. "Tamera, I don't really want to be Juliet," she said.

"You don't?"

Tia shook her head. "I never really wanted the part. How do I have the time to learn a major role in a play as well as get this project finished?"

"So why did you say you'd do it?"

Tia shrugged. "I thought it might be the one thing that made you wake up and get back to normal. Boy, was I scared when I thought I'd be stuck with it."

"But you are stuck with it," Tamera said. "Damien would never let me have the part back now."

"He might if you went to him and apologized," Tia said. "After all, you were his number one choice for Juliet."

Tamera shook her head. "I don't think I could face them again. That creep Danielle hates my guts."

Tia patted her sister's shoulder. "Tamera, if you really want to be an actress some day, you're going to have to get used to other actresses hating your guts. It's part of the profession. Go back there, only this time don't give them a reason to hate you."

Tamera sat staring out across the room. "You really think that Damien might let me come back?"

"You can only try asking him," Tia said. "What have you got to lose? If you really want to be in the play again, that is."

"I really do," Tamera said. "I know I said all that stuff about the play stinking, but I didn't really mean it."

"I know," Tia said.

"I've got a great idea," Tamera said. "I can get my part back, and we don't need to tell anybody. I can pretend to be you. That way I won't have to face Damien and Danielle and all those people."

"Oh no," Tia said, shaking her head. "Bad things always happen when we switch places, Tamera. You have to apologize to Damien. If you don't, he'll go on thinking badly of you, and you wouldn't want that, would you?"

"I guess not," Tamera said. "Okay, I'll go to Damien tomorrow. Although I'm not looking forward to it one bit."

"That will make Lamar very happy," Tia said.

"Really? You really think I've still got a chance with him, Tia?"

"Of course you've still got a chance, Tamera. He

likes you. He was desperate to try to come up with a way to snap you out of your craziness."

Tamera sighed. "I feel so much better," she said. "If you ever see me start acting stupidly again . . ."

"Don't worry," Tia said. "I'll hit you over the head, drag you home, and lock you in your room until you wise up."

"Thank you," Tamera answered. "Now, do you want to start putting this model together again? You read how it should go and I'll stack the blocks."

"Thanks, but I think I'd better work on it alone," Tia said. "No offense, but . . ."

"I know, I stink at science," Tamera said. "But I don't even care, just as long as I get one more chance to be a great actress."

The next afternoon Tamera waited for Damien outside the auditorium. The moment she saw him, she ran over to him.

"Can I talk to you, please?" she asked.

"Sure, Tia. What's up?" he said pleasantly.

"I'm not Tia, I'm Tamera," she said. She watched the smile leave Damien's face as he looked at her warily.

"Look, Tamera, I'm really busy right now," he said. "Rehearsal starts in one minute."

"This will only take a minute," Tamera said. She took a deep breath. "I came to tell you I was sorry. I acted like a jerk."

Damien looked surprised. "You sure did," he said.

"I don't know what got into me," Tamera went

on. "I'm not normally that kind of person. In fact I hate people who throw their weight around and act like snobs. I guess I was so amazed at getting the lead in the play that it fried my brains."

Damien smiled. "I guess that stardom has gone to a lot of actors' heads before now."

Tamera bit her lip nervously. "I just wondered if you'd give me another chance if I promised to behave better this time."

"Tamera, I don't know what to say," he said. "I already offered the part to your sister, and she's doing a good job."

"My sister doesn't really want the part," Tamera said. "We talked about it last night. She only took it to try to shake me out of my craziness. Right now she'd rather be working on her science fair project."

There was a long pause before Damien said, "Okay, Tamera. I'm prepared to give you another chance. Only this time—"

"I know," Tamera said. "No interrupting, no thinking that I know better than you, and I say the words just as they're written."

Damien grinned. "You got it," he said. He moved closer to her. "I'll let you into a little secret, Tamera. I took a big risk giving you the part in the first place. Everyone else wanted Danielle to be Juliet. She was the obvious choice. She's a terrific actress. But I saw you sitting there, and you looked to me exactly how I imagined Juliet."

Tamera stood there, letting this sink in. Damien hadn't chosen her for her great acting ability in the first place. He'd chosen her because she looked right. In which case, Tia looked equally right. She found herself feeling very small and stupid.

"This time I'll really try hard," Tamera said. "I won't let you down, Damien."

Damien looked at her and a smile spread across his face. "Okay, Tamera, you got it," he said.

"And Damien, one little thing—"

"Yes, Tamera?" Damien asked suspiciously.

"Please don't tell the others right away. Let me tell them. I'd like to apologize to them, too."

"All right, if that's what you really want," Damien said. "Now, get in there and work like crazy. We've only got two weeks to get this show on the road!"

Tamera took several deep breaths before she went on to the stage. She went over to a chair in the corner and studied her lines. She had stayed up very late the night before, reading them over and over, in case Damien let her play Juliet again. This time she didn't want to make any mistakes.

"Hi, Tia," Danielle said as she passed Tamera's chair.

Tamera opened her mouth, but Danielle went right on. "You know, Tia, I can't tell you how glad I am that you took over as Juliet. I know Tamera is your sister, but she was such a pain. Now she's gone, everything is going just fine, and you're going to be great as Juliet."

There was a long pause, then Tamera said, "Thank you, Danielle. I'll try my best."

"I know you will," Danielle said, giving her a warm smile.

Why didn't you tell her? Tamera asked herself angrily as Danielle walked away. She's going to have to know sometime. But not right now, she added.

Then she saw Lamar. He looked so handsome that it almost took her breath away. She wanted to run right up to him and fling her arms around him and beg his forgiveness, but she made herself go on sitting quietly with her script as he passed her.

"Hi, Tia," he said. "How are you coming along with your lines?"

"Okay, thanks," Tamera muttered, not wanting to look up and meet his eyes.

"Places everybody. Run-through of act one," Damien called, clapping his hands.

Tamera got up and stood in the wings, ready for her first entrance. She went through the scene with the nurse and her mother. Then she watched Romeo come onto the stage. Finally she was alone with him. As they said the lines to each other, she saw a puzzled expression come over Lamar's face. The moment came when he had to take her in his arms. As his arms came around her and she looked up into his face, she saw his eyes light up. He said his line and then kissed her. It wasn't like a stage kiss at all.

Chapter 13

ᗄᗄ

*T*amera managed to get through the rest of the scene. As she came offstage she saw Lamar still looking at her.

"Hi—uh, Tia," he said, his eyes teasing hers.

"Did you know it was me, or do you always kiss my sister like that?" Tamera demanded, her eyes teasing his now.

"You'll never know," he said, chuckling. "Do the others know it's you?"

"Only Damien. I went to see him and apologized," Tamera said. "I want to apologize to everyone else, too, but I couldn't face them all at once." She looked up at Lamar shyly. "I'd like to start with you, Lamar."

Before she could say anything more, Damien leaped up onto the stage. "Good job, everyone. Excellent," he said. "Romeo and Juliet—that was a steamy scene there."

"You'd better not let Tamera hear about this, Tia," one of the guys teased. "He never kissed her like that."

Tamera saw Damien looking at her. "Actually, I'm not Tia, I'm Tamera," she said. "We switched back again."

"Sure you are," the boy said. "As if Damien would let Tamera come back again."

"No, seriously," Tamera said.

"You can't be Tamera," the boy said. "You knew your lines. You stood in the right places, and you didn't tell everyone else how to act their parts."

"Maybe I'm the new, improved Tamera," she said.

Lamar touched her arm. "Let them think what they like," he said. "Why don't you wait until the cast party to set them straight? It will be easier on you."

"Okay," Tamera said.

The rehearsal went on. Tamera said all her lines perfectly. At the end Damien came over to her. "If I tell you that you were good, you won't let it go to your head, will you?" he asked.

"Never again," Tamera said. "I've learned my lesson the hard way. I can't believe that I nearly lost my big chance." She looked across at Lamar. And I nearly lost the sweetest guy in the world, she thought.

She went up to him. "Do you have a moment, Lamar?" she said. "I'd really like to talk for a while."

"Sure," he said. "Do you want to go somewhere in my car?"

"The park would be fine," Tamera said as they walked out into the parking lot together. "I know that's a favorite hangout of yours."

"How do you know that?" he asked, smiling at her.

"I saw you there with my sister. I jumped to the wrong conclusion and boy, was I mad," she said.

"Tia was worried about you," Lamar said. "So was I."

"I know that now," Tamera said. "You are both so nice to care about me. I know I don't deserve it, the way I've been acting."

They got into Lamar's car. A few minutes later they stopped by the duck pond, where Tamera had seen Lamar and Tia.

"You want to walk?" Lamar asked.

Tamera nodded. "I wish I'd brought the rest of my lunch to feed the ducks."

"They're fat enough," Lamar said, smiling. "Little kids and old ladies feed them all day."

They started walking around the pond.

"Lamar, this is hard for me, but I wanted to tell you how sorry I am," Tamera said. "I still can't believe the way I behaved. But like Tia said, the spell is broken now. I'm back to being my old self, and I promise I'll never act like a stuck-up snob again." Shyly she took his hand. "You are the best thing that's ever happened to me, Lamar. I can't believe I nearly blew it with you. Will you give me another chance?"

"I might," Lamar said slowly. "Although I'm not sure that a girlfriend like you is right for my image as a future acting star. I need someone who is as famous and good looking as me. I thought maybe that Brandy would be better. . . ."

"Shut up!" Tamera said, laughing. "I'm being serious, Lamar. I need to know if I've still got a chance with you."

Lamar slipped his arms around her waist. "I'm willing to give it another try, Tamera. But I want you to understand one thing."

"What's that?"

"Tia and I . . ."

"Yes?"

"We've become good friends. I really like talking to her, Tamera. So if you ever see me with Tia, I don't want you to be jealous."

"I see," Tamera said hesitantly.

"But just because I like talking to Tia doesn't mean that I want her as a girlfriend. She's just a friend, nothing more."

"And me?" Tamera whispered.

"Not just a friend," Lamar said. They stood there, gazing into each other's eyes until their lips came together in a long, warm kiss.

Two weeks later *Romeo and Juliet* had its opening night. Lisa prepared an early meal, but Tamera was too nervous to eat.

"Eat something, baby. You've got a whole lot of words to say up on that stage," Lisa urged. "Here, try some of this Jell-O salad. It just slips down."

"Thanks," Tamera said, and tried to swallow the

spoonful that Lisa held out to her, "but I'm really not hungry, Lisa."

"What are you having, Ray?" Lisa asked, picking up his plate to serve him. "You're not eating either."

"Me? I'm so nervous, I couldn't eat a thing," Ray said. "It's my baby's opening night. I'm so excited I could burst."

Tamera caught Tia's eye across the table and grinned at her. It felt great to have her father feeling proud of her for a change.

"I tell you what," Ray said. "Why don't we forget about this meal and all go out for dinner after the show?"

"I've got the opening night party after the show, Dad," Tamera said.

"That's okay, baby. Then we'll go out some other night," Ray said. "I'll book a table at the best restaurant in town. I'll have us driven there in my biggest limousine. Maybe we'll tip off the press that you're going to be there—it will be great publicity for you."

"Maybe they'll give us a discount because she's a celebrity," Lisa suggested.

Tamera shook her head. "Thanks, but I'd rather just go to our favorite pizza place," she said. "No more acting like somebody I'm not. I just want to be plain old Tamera Campbell from now on, enjoying my family and friends."

"I'm with you, honey," Lisa said. "The eentsy-weentsy portions they give you at those fancy places aren't enough to fill up a flea."

A car horn sounded outside. Tamera jumped up. "That will be Lamar," she said. "I have to go."

Ray got up and hugged her. "Good luck, honey. Knock them dead," he said.

"Break a leg, Tamera," Lisa said, hugging her in turn. "And try to speak those lines so that I can understand a few of them, okay? Or your dad will have to keep pinching me to stop me from falling asleep."

"Don't worry, I'll pinch her," Tia said.

Tamera stood in front of Tia. "Good luck," Tia said softly. "I know you're going to be just great."

"Thanks," Tamera said, feeling a big lump coming into her throat. "Thanks for everything, Tia. I couldn't have done it without you. You are definitely the world's greatest sister."

"Can I have that in writing?" Tia asked. "It might be useful the next time I won't let you borrow my clothes."

Tamera laughed as she ran out of the front door. Lamar got out of the car to meet her. "Hi, Juliet," he said softly.

"Hi, Romeo."

"These are for you," Lamar said. He handed her a bouquet of red roses.

"Oh, wow," Tamera stammered. "I don't know what to say. It's the first time in my whole life that anyone has given me flowers."

"You'd better get used to it," Lamar said. "Famous actresses get flowers all the time."

"I don't want to get used to it, ever," Tamera said,

climbing into the car, holding her bouquet close to her. "I want to feel as special as I do right now. Thank you, Lamar." She leaned across and kissed his cheek. Lamar gave her an embarrassed smile.

As she stood in the wings, ready to make her first entrance, Tamera was so nervous that she found it hard to breathe. When she tried to think of her opening line, her mind was blank. Her throat felt so dry that she was sure no sound would come out, even if she could remember her line.

"There's a great crowd out there," Damien whispered, putting a friendly hand on Tamera's shoulder. "Break a leg, everyone."

The curtain went up on the opening scene. There was a round of applause. Then it was Tamera's turn. She stepped out into the spotlight and heard the applause. She opened her mouth and words came out. Suddenly she wasn't Tamera, remembering lines— she was a young girl called Juliet who lived long, long ago.

When she and Lamar came forward to make their final bow, the applause was deafening. Lamar squeezed her hand and smiled at her. In the front row she could see her father and Lisa and Tia, all smiling up at her with proud, happy faces. Nothing had ever felt so good in Tamera's whole life. She had finally done something she could be proud of. She couldn't believe how close she had come to wrecking it.

The curtain fell and the actors hugged each other excitedly.

Before Tamera knew it, she was hugging Roger. "Congratulations, Tamera. You were good," Roger said.

Danielle was standing close enough to overhear. "What are you talking about?" she demanded. "She's Tia, not Tamera."

"I know Tamera when I see her," Roger said, beaming at Tamera. "I've been studying her, in detail, since she was ten years old." He patted Tamera's hand. "I'll be waiting to dance with you at the cast party, my little flower."

Tamera could feel Danielle staring at her as Roger walked away. "You really are Tamera, not Tia?" she snapped. "I've been nice to Tamera all this time?"

Tamera put on her best actress expression. "That's something you'll never know, Danielle," she said, and swept past her to join Lamar and her family.

About the Author

Janet Quin-Harkin has written over fifty books for teenagers, including the best-seller *Ten-Boy Summer*. She is the author of several popular series: TGIF!, Friends, Heartbreak Café, Senior Year, and The Boyfriend Club. She has also written several romances.

Ms. Quin-Harkin lives with her husband in San Rafael, California. She has four children. In addition to writing books, she teaches creative writing at a nearby college.

R.L. STINE'S
GHOSTS OF FEAR STREET®

1 HIDE AND SHRIEK 52941-2/$3.99
2 WHO'S BEEN SLEEPING IN MY GRAVE? 52942-0/$3.99
3 THE ATTACK OF THE AQUA APES 52943-9/$3.99
4 NIGHTMARE IN 3-D 52944-7/$3.99
5 STAY AWAY FROM THE TREE HOUSE 52945-5/$3.99
6 EYE OF THE FORTUNETELLER 52946-3/$3.99
7 FRIGHT KNIGHT 52947-1/$3.99
8 THE OOZE 52948-X/$3.99
9 REVENGE OF THE SHADOW PEOPLE 52949-8/$3.99
10 THE BUGMAN LIVES! 52950-1/$3.99
11 THE BOY WHO ATE FEAR STREET 00183-3/$3.99
12 NIGHT OF THE WERECAT 00184-1/$3.99
13 HOW TO BE A VAMPIRE 00185-X/$3.99
14 BODY SWITCHERS FROM OUTER SPACE 00186-8/$3.99
15 FRIGHT CHRISTMAS 00187-6/$3.99
16 DON'T EVER GET SICK AT GRANNY'S 00188-4/$3.99
17 HOUSE OF A THOUSAND SCREAMS 00190-6/$3.99
18 CAMP FEAR GHOULS 00191-4/$3.99
19 THREE EVIL WISHES 00189-2/$3.99

Available from Minstrel® Books
Published by Pocket Books

POCKET BOOKS

FOR MORE LAUGHS

TUNE IN TO

Sister Sister

ON THE
WB TELEVISION
NETWORK